Banshee Song

Blood Fae Chronicles
Book 2

USA TODAY BEST SELLING AUTHOR
Jen Katemi

Contents

Banshee Song (The Blood Fae Chronicles)
Copyright © 2020 Jen Katemi
All rights reserved

ISBN-13: 978-0-6484045-6-9

First Print Edition
Published by Jen Katemi (Flourish Books)

Chapter One

INDIGO

The last note dies away and silence fills the theater. The quality of that silence is sharp and expectant, as if everyone in the audience is holding their breath and waiting for more.

There is no more. Not for these humans. If I truly gave them everything I have, there would be no silence, only terrified screams, and the rush of bodies toward the exit. Away from the horror. Away from me.

Slowly the applause begins, escalating as the audience rises to their feet. A standing ovation. I must have excelled tonight. I lift my chin and gaze out past the stage lights to acknowledge the accolades directed my way.

"Bravo, brava, huzzah..."

The shouts vary from person to person, but all convey essentially the same message. I delivered what this audience wanted, and then some.

"Encore, encore..."

I incline my head, blinking hard to force back the threatening tears. Do they know I sing of death? Do they know I sing of loss and all things that might be and never eventuate? Do they know how much it costs me, every time I stand up here on this stage, to croon the song of every human passing?

The power of a banshee's voice is beyond the understanding of all of them, mortal and immortal alike.

Of course, I'm only a half-banshee. Even so, I have to rein in my voice to deliver as much as they can take, and not a single note more.

The threat of tears eases and this time when I raise my head, confidence fills me. Tonight will be okay. There is no one nearby who needs the call of the banshee this evening.

As I take one more bow and turn to leave the stage, a spark of silver from someone in the front row catches and holds my attention. A set of steel-gray eyes meet mine, and for the briefest moment my heart does a strange flip-flop in my chest. A tall man—taller than those around him by at least a head—continues to slow clap in what seems like a parody of the adulation around him.

His hair is dark and long, pulled back in an elegant ponytail. Like everyone else I can see in the limited reach of the stage lights, he's sporting evening wear, but this man gives off the impression that he is only here under sufferance.

The sparkle emanates from a ring on one of his fingers. Another flash from the piece of jewellery sets my heart fluttering again. Who is he? And why is he looking at me that way, as if he knows me and doesn't like what he sees?

The sardonic twist of his lips sends a different message altogether to the continued and almost offensive slow clap.

I'm certain, even in the glance I give him before leaving the stage, that he's not human.

Elf? Fae? The slightly pointed ears, aristocratic nose, and high cheekbones could be either, but elves are usually light-haired, not dark, which means this guy is likely pure fae.

Awesome. If there's anything I hate more than a cynical man, it's a cynical man with fae blood running through his veins.

I nod graciously and give him a twisted smile of my own. *See, faerie man? I can do sarcastic, too.*

A flash centers in those hard, silver-gray eyes. He received my message, all right. The impact of that glare and the resultant heat in my veins follows me all the way back to my dressing room.

For once, I'm grateful for the empty room. In the past, back when I was part of the chorus and had to fight nineteen other women for space in front of the mirror, I dreamed of being a star and having my own dressing area where people would leave me in peace unless I chose to invite them in to my little sanctuary.

Be careful what you wish for. Now that I have exactly what I always dreamed of, I can't bear to be alone for a moment longer than absolutely necessary. Not since Sienna... *No. Don't think of her. It's fine. You have a voice far stronger than most, and one call will bring them all running. You're not alone. Not really.*

I take a seat and stare at my reflection in the dresser mirror. My haunted green eyes stare back, and I blink a few times and force deep breaths, aiming for calm. *There. That's better. Under control once again. Push the pain back where it belongs, deep down inside where it can't get out and hurt you.*

Or anyone else.

My blonde hair is loose and flowing in waves over my shoulders and partway down my back. The red dress is as low-cut as it can get without spilling my naked breasts out for all to see. The audience calls for seductive in this industry, and seductive is what I deliver. The blonde is merely a wig, hiding my natural dark color, but in this business, blonde is considered far sexier than any other color and I need all the advantages I can get. I haven't been brunette on stage for at least ten years. Probably more.

I slide off the wig, followed by the underlying wig cap and pins, and run my fingers through my real hair, shaking it loose. The freedom feels good. Whenever I leave the theater, dark-haired and make-up free, I am thankfully unrecognizable from the siren they all see on stage.

I take a wipe from the container on the dresser, and have only just begun to swipe the heavy stage makeup from my eyes and lips when a decisive knock at the door stays my hand. I stifle a sigh. While I normally encourage visitors after a show to keep the shadows at bay, tonight, I specifically asked my assistant not to let anyone through. There's a lethargy, deep in my bones, that I can't explain. I don't think it's a banshee call. It feels different than the stretched, agonizing build-up of pain that denotes a song of death.

Maybe I'm coming down with flu? Whatever the issue is, I just need to go home and sleep.

And now, I have one eye still fully made up and the other smeared with half-removed eyeliner. My red lipstick is smeared all the way across, *a la* Joker. *Awesome.* Whoever is at the door will have to suck it up because I'm too tired to care right now. Most likely it's Dreya, my assistant.

"It's open, Dreya, love. Come on—*oh!*"

The door opens before I've even finished and the stranger from the audience strides into the room as if he owns the space. Instantly, my dressing room seems far too small, as if his very presence sucks out all the air. He towers above me and I stand, trying to minimize the height difference between us. My stupid, traitorous heart pounds. What is it about this fae that causes my body to react in such an intense manner?

He stares around the room, peering into every corner with a suspicious air, before he turns that gaze back onto me. His almost-concealed recoil confirms that I must, indeed, look rather clown-like.

"What are you searching for? There are no hidden surprises or secret admirers stashed away behind a rack of costumes. I *am* actually alone in here, you know." My voice comes out testier than I want, and I clear my throat and try again. "Okay. Can I help you?"

He lets out a tiny snort. "I doubt it. But perhaps *I* can help *you*, Indigo."

My name shivers off his tongue and raises goosebumps along my skin. "Who are you?"

He doesn't answer. Instead, he hooks a foot around the leg of the chair I just vacated and shifts it forward. "Take a seat, and we'll talk."

"No, I'm good right here, thanks." I cross my arms in front of my chest, wishing like hell I hadn't half swiped off my makeup and that, instead, I had first opted to change into more modest clothing. "I'll ask again. Who are you, faerie man, and what do you want? You're clearly not a fan, given your insulting behavior in the audience."

"Faerie man?" The indignation in his tone is somewhat satisfying and I fight a sudden urge to grin. He matches my stance, crossing his arms in front of an impressively wide chest. "I am Tarrien, Lord and Warrior of the Winter Court, and I am here at your mother's behest to offer you protection."

Wait. What? I wasn't expecting *that*. I can't help the laugh that escapes me. So many questions rise up.

"My *mother* sent you? Are you serious?"

He arches a winged brow. "Of course. I would not joke about such a thing."

Of course, he wouldn't. He looks like he doesn't have a humorous bone in his body.

"Protection from what? And, by the way, I haven't seen my mother in, like, forever, and I've been taking care of myself since I left the foster care system at sixteen. I don't need her help, or your protection. At all."

"Foster care?"

"Yeah. It's for kids who have no family and nowhere to live."

His head tips to one side. "Hmm. Your mother has a lot to answer for, that is true."

I release a sigh, the tiredness spreading through my body. "I don't need protection, thank you. You've had a wasted trip."

I point toward the door, but he doesn't take the hint.

Instead, he studies me intently. "You look much more attractive with dark hair. More like your mother. Only, you do not seem like her at all, except on the surface. That is a good thing."

I ignore the first part of that sentence, which causes a strange flip-flop in my chest, and concentrate on the latter part.

"Not like my dear old mum? The woman who ran out when I was only a month or so old, and came back when I was seven to tell me how important I am because I'm half-banshee. And then told me I have another name—something really long and unpronounceable—before telling me I can never reveal it? And then, turned around and disappeared once again, just like that?" I huff out a breath. "You mean, *that* woman? Damn right I'm nothing like her!"

My legs choose this moment to develop the shakes, and despite my earlier comment about wanting to stand, I drop into the chair. "You're a fae warrior. From the Winter Court? And she sent you to protect me... from what?"

He squats down in front of me until we're at eye level. Far from reducing his presence and size, the proximity serves to emphasize it. I look down, away from the intensity in his expression, and notice instead how muscled his thighs are, and how tight those trousers are around his groin. Gods above, I'm acting as if I haven't had sex in years. *Which, I guess, I haven't.* I quickly squelch that thought. It's beside the point.

I lift my gaze straight back up and focus somewhere over his left shoulder.

"Danger has arrived in this world, Indigo. Danger to all humans, and most especially to those of the hybrid human-banshee variety, like yourself. The Lady Renna bade me protect you. It is what I do, after all. I am a Winter Warrior and I am bound to my duty." His lips tighten briefly. "Whether I wish to be, or not."

"Okay..." I'm not really sure how to respond. Clearly, this assignment is not to his liking. "What, specifically, is the danger you're supposed to protect me from?"

His brows come together in a scowl. "I do not know, exactly. But one of Renna's other daughters—your half-sister Aleah—almost died several days ago after an attack, and your mother has become concerned for your welfare."

I almost laugh at the absurdity of that last statement, but the rest of it is too bizarre to allow for humor. I know I have half-siblings out there somewhere—lots of them from what my mother told me when she visited many years ago—but to finally hear the actual name of one of them makes things all the more real.

"Aleah." I try out the name, liking the sound of it. I wonder if she's anything like me. "Is she okay?"

"Yes. When I left her, she was wrapped naked around a vampire police officer, about to have the best sex of her life, by the look of them."

Good for her! I raise a brow. "Not in too much danger, then."

"Aleah came as close to death as it is possible to do, without crossing over the line. She almost had your mother calling in her death. Without my healing power back in Faerie, your sister would not now be able to enjoy her cozy liaison with her vampire lover."

"Healing power? I thought you were a warrior."

"I am." He appears offended. "Are you not familiar with the extent of a Court Warrior's power? Our hearts may be encased in ice, but we fight to protect, and we fight to heal."

What does he mean, his heart is encased in ice? Does that mean he cannot feel? Cannot love? There are times I would give *anything* not to feel. When the banshee call arrives, the extent of what I feel almost tears me in two. But never to love? Never to experience any true emotion?

I can't imagine a worse fate.

Pity for the man squatting before me begins to stir in my chest, and I lock it back down before it can take off. He does not seem like the type who would appreciate being pitied.

"Look." I stand up, intending to sidle around him toward the door. "I do know many things about the fae world, and about banshees. My mother spent a month talking non-stop about it all when I last saw her. But I was *seven*, Tarrien. Seven years old. That's a long time ago. I'm *thirty-one* now. I can't remember everything she said back then, and even if I could, I pretty much doubt she mentioned you at all. Fae do seem to have an inflated sense of ego, that much is certain. She talked mainly about herself!"

I push past him, intending to head for the door and

insist that he leave, when my leg accidentally brushes against his knee. A zing of hot energy pulses right through me. I feel it from my hair follicles right down to my red-painted toenails.

"Whoa! What the—"

He leaps to his feet, the movement much faster and lighter than I expect from such a strongly built guy, and he takes a step back and away. He opens and closes his mouth, as if about to speak but not quite sure what to say. Confusion reigns on his features.

So, he felt that, too. Maybe it's only his emotions encased in ice, not his man bits. From the looks of him, he's about as happy about that strange zing as I am. Which is to say, not happy at all.

"Okay, I think it's time for you to leave, Tarrien. I appreciate the offer, but as I've already stated, I don't want or need your protection. You can let my mother know I'm perfectly fine on my own."

No, you're not. The little voice deep in my brain tries to make itself heard, but I shut it down before all the bad stuff can rise up and leach out once again.

"I don't believe you understand—"

"I'm not sure why you're here doing my mother's bidding," I cut across him. "I'm aware she has the favor of the Winter King for some reason—she told me that daily when she visited—but I didn't realize she could command iced up warriors to work for her. I thank you, but the answer is still, no thanks."

I am not having this guy follow me around to

interfere in my everyday life. After what happened a few months ago, I'm determined to get back to my own brand of "normal" as soon as I can. *If* I can.

Sienna's death was not your fault.

My therapist's words echo in my head. *It would be beneficial to get back to as many of your normal routines and activities as you can, Indigo. Live your life as you always have. And let the self-blame go.*

I blink, bringing my attention back to the present. Tarrien glares at me in a way that communicates heat rather than ice. I wonder if he's aware of that. Is his heart figuratively encased in ice, or literally? If the latter, what happens if someone gets him all het up? Will the ice melt?

What happens when he has sex? *Does* he ever have sex? I wrap my arms across my middle, willing myself to stop thinking about sex and Tarrien.

"I'm not giving you a choice, Indigo." His tone is stern.

"Damn right you are, faerie man. This is *my* life. And now it's time for you to leave."

I open the door and call out for my assistant. Dreya is the best dresser in Melbourne and I'm lucky she enjoys working with me.

"Yes, Indie?" she says, stepping into the doorway of the room. "Do you need..." She peers past me and her mouth drops open.

After a minute I reach out and tap her chin to remind her to close it.

"Are you sure you want *him* out of here?" Her whisper is almost silent, but not enough to avoid a fae's acute hearing, I'm sure.

The faint snort behind me confirms it.

"This is Tarrien, who has outstayed his welcome," I say. "Kindly ensure he is seen off the premises immediately. Thank you, Dreya."

"Okay, if you insist." She shrugs and leans out into the hallway, making a surreptitious gesture. Instantly two burly security guards are at her side. "This gentleman is leaving. Mistress Indigo is indisposed."

And nuts, she mouths, waggling her eyebrows. *He's hot*.

I roll my eyes at her, and step away from the door. After a moment in which I wonder if Tarrien will protest, he narrows his eyes and glares at me.

"You don't know what you're doing, you stupid banshee." With a quick movement, he darts to my dressing table and picks up a makeup wipe. For a large man he is remarkably graceful. "Maybe clean the rest of your face. You look ridiculous. Unfortunately for us both, I will see you again. And soon."

Stupid banshee? Ridiculous? I open my mouth to give him a serve of my best vitriol. He touches a silver ring that decorates his thumb in a delicate filigree circle, and vanishes, just like that, leaving me seething with a mixture of fury and something baser. Something that curls through my system and warms me in secret places I haven't thought about for a long while. Something that I don't want to label.

Something that I definitely don't want to feel, for a man who has just called me stupid.

I blink a few times, aiming for calm. *Well. That was unexpected.*

"Are you all right, Indie?" Dreya peers around me, searching the room just as Tarrien did when he first arrived. *Seriously.* My dressing room is not that big. "He might have been hot to look at, but I guess he was just another dickhead."

"Indeed." *Dickhead.* Yes, that's exactly the right word for Tarrien. I smile at Dreya, sharing a girl moment, and repeating that word in my head until my anger at the unexpected intrusion dissipates.

Dreya confirms with the theater security guards that they are no longer required, and then turns back to study me after they leave. "Would you like me to come home with you, tonight, Indie? Just to make sure the weirdo isn't lurking anywhere outside your apartment?"

"I'm fine, Drey love." I keep my voice light, but I'm not okay, and we both know it. I haven't been okay for months, not since the attack. I don't know if I'll ever be fine again.

I do know how to look after myself, though. My banshee heritage gives me some enhanced capabilities over a full human, including strength, hearing, and sight. Dreya, one-hundred percent human like Sienna was, is therefore more fragile than me. And that makes it doubly sweet of her to offer assistance.

She continues to stare at me with a raised brow.

"Thank you, but no," I say. "He was just a pesky annoyance from the fae realm, and hopefully, he's gone back there to sulk and find someone else to annoy."

Dreya is aware of my half-fae bloodline, and unlike many humans who display speciesism, she has no issue with my heritage. "If you're sure..."

"I am. Let me finish getting changed, and then can you call my driver, please? Say, fifteen minutes?"

It's not far to my apartment in East Melbourne, but one of the perks of being the star attraction in this theater troupe, is the driver and town car at my beck and call. I used to walk home after the late show, but these days I prefer the safety inherent in the back seat of a car, so I call upon the driver far more than I used to.

"Sure. Will do. And I know you said no visitors tonight, Indie. I didn't let him past; I swear."

"I know that. Just arrange my driver, love, and I'll be happy."

When I sit back at the dressing table, I can't deny that I do look rather ridiculous with one eye and my lips smeared halfway across my face. Still, it was unbelievably rude of him to point it out.

I just want to be at home in my cozy little sanctuary —the safest place I know—and curl up in a ball in my king-sized bed to block out the rest of the world. The lethargy is growing, and I don't want to face what that might mean.

One night of peace. Please give me that, universe. Please. No deaths.

I don't think I have the strength to face a banshee call tonight.

Chapter Two

TARRIEN

I should not have called the banshee hybrid *stupid*. Clearly, she is not. That was discourteous and now I owe her an apology for that. Yet Indigo is proving to be as annoying as her mother and when her green eyes flashed at me with such disregard, the ill-mannered words simply fell out of my mouth.

I should have given her more information about the abominations and what happened to her sister, Aleah. I thought to introduce the threat more gradually, to avoid any unnecessary panic. Now, I see that perhaps she would be more receptive to straight-talk. I will try that tactic, when I see her again.

Why will she not simply accept that I wish to protect her? Why will she not take my word for it that the danger is real and potentially headed her way?

Annoyance fills me, together with something baser that my mind veers away from labelling.

I didn't expect her to be so hauntingly beautiful. Sure, she's half-fae, but I *live* in Faerie. I mix with both full-bloods and hybrids on a daily basis, so it isn't her banshee-human combination that sends my senses into overdrive. Renna is a renowned beauty but that woman leaves me cold. Frozen wasteland cold. I am the perfect winter warrior when Renna is near. Her very presence ensures my heart remains encased in the ice that is supposed to keep my actions pure.

The moment I laid eyes on Indigo—when she began to sing with the voice of an angel like the diva she is—my warrior blood heated in a way it never has before. Her green eyes stared down at me from the theater stage in what looked like contempt. A curl of her beautiful, blood-red lips cemented that effect.

Her blonde hair was stunning enough, while she sang. But seeing her real hair—those thick dark waves cascading down her back—almost had me sinking my fingers into the delicious sea of darkness as soon as I entered her dressing room.

I had to concentrate to keep my hands to myself and my gaze off those lush, ripe breasts almost spilling out of the tight red dress. The outfit was clearly designed to reel in men of all species and to keep us suspended on the edge of reason as we imagine sinking our faces into her cleavage and tasting the delicious, pale flesh on offer.

And more than that—inciting us to want to *own* that flesh. Take possession in a way that would send the contempt on her face spinning into non-existence and eliciting a full-throated cry of passion that would let loose for the whole world to hear.

A banshee cry. All mine.

Fuck.

I rub my temples, washing away the beginnings of a headache. I need to be better than this. Desire is not supposed to be this difficult to avoid. I am a winter warrior, I remind myself. My heart is protected from the heat of passion for a reason. If I succumb, I cannot fulfil my duties of protection and healing as effectively as I need to.

Look at what happened when Father gave in to his needs.

Right now, with the banshee hybrid in denial about the growing threat of violence and death, I need to keep my power at full strength.

I have to shut down my emotions and my physical attraction to Indigo if I want to protect her. And I *have* to protect her, if I ever want to be free of this incessant debt that my family owes to Renna. Stay focused on the task and perhaps my father will not be executed or go to prison when he is caught.

Prison in Faerie is nothing like prison in this realm. My father would not survive the rigors of those winter cells in the dungeons beneath the palace, I am sure of it. And if my father passed from existence, I know my mother would soon follow suit. Despite the fact that what he has already done has destroyed her life and that of our whole family, she still loves him and holds a kernel of hope for his return.

Damn my father. And damn Indigo, for being such an enticing, stubborn, annoying little wench. I won't succumb to her hybrid charm. I *can't*.

Not if I want to do my duty and keep her safe from the abominations.

Now, I will have to secretly follow her home and somehow ensure her continued safety, without her cooperation.

Indigo

HOME IS where the heart is, and for me, that's my black and white cat, Lola. She turned up one night just after Sienna died, at a time I needed her most, and has stayed ever since, sleeping by my side and within reach whenever a banshee call tears my body and my emotions apart.

"Hey, girl. Want some supper?"

We have a routine. When I get home from a show, invariably well past midnight, she's waiting. I arrange her supper first, and then have mine before we cuddle up together on the couch while I de-stress with some internet surfing on my laptop.

We are mid-routine, fed and happily curled up on

the couch with Lola's purr vibrating against my thigh, when I feel the beginnings of a call.

Oh, God. No, no, no. Not tonight. I don't have enough energy. Not tonight. *Please*, not tonight.

The lethargy I experienced earlier has delivered a present I do not want to accept.

Too bad I don't have a choice. The agony rushes in and the wail builds, the force of it pushing up and out of my throat in a pulse of energy that carries the call of the banshee out into the night air.

I begin to cry as if my heart is about to break, the sobs uncontrolled, the pain centering in my gut. Who is it? What is happening to them? Why, oh why must I live the agony and sadness of death, over and over and over?

Is it someone I know? Can I do something to help? To warn them? *Something!*

Lola is already standing sentinel, alert and waiting to see what I need from her. I stagger to my feet and head toward the front door. Lola follows, biting at one of my ankles. She obviously doesn't want me to leave the apartment, but this agony is beyond the norm. The strength of the call means it must be someone close by. If it is someone in the apartment building, then chances are it is a neighbor. I might know them, at least a little.

I don't have a choice. I have to do *something*. I have to try and help.

I have no idea how I reach the elevator but I

manage to push the button before another wave hits. Oh, my God, the pain. What is happening? Whoever is going through this is probably a hundred times more desperate than me. I hit the button for floor six. The agony feels like it is coming from above, and there is only one floor above mine on level five.

When I stagger out a few seconds later, I know I'm correct. Blood spatters line the hallway, from the elevator all the way to one of the apartments on the right. The door is wide open—most unusual for anyone living in the city—and I belatedly try to pull my phone from the pocket of my pajama top to call for assistance. It's not there. My phone must be still downstairs in my apartment.

Pain explodes in my head. I gasp and let out another wail before falling to my knees. Is whoever is doing this to my neighbor still in there? Will this be the end for me? Is this the death that will finally end up killing me, too?

I'm not stopping now, though. I've come too far to give up. I begin to crawl on hands and knees, passing a hall table on which a vase of fake flowers rests. I scrabble, pulling myself up the leg of the table until I reach the vase. I tip the flowers out and smash the vase itself, grabbing a piece of broken pottery in my hand.

Not much of a weapon, but it is better than going in empty-handed.

Plus, I have my voice. That is a weapon in itself. As

a fresh wave of agony hits, I finally stop holding back. I let loose the true song of the banshee.

My voice rises to such a level that glass shatters nearby. I stagger forward and the volume of my song increases, the notes becoming higher and purer, the nearer I get to the open door.

Another door opens further down the hallway and a horrified male face peeps out briefly, hands covering his ears, before quickly disappearing. *Get help. Call for help. Now.*

I hope the neighbor is racing to their phone. I hope someone already has called the cops. If not, I'm likely going to be as dead as whoever is dying in that room ahead, within the next couple of minutes.

I reach the door just as the pain dissipates into nothing. The dying person, whoever they were, has left this earthly plane. I collapse completely onto the ground, curling into the foetal position. I somehow manage to roll onto my side so I can peer into the room. I wish I hadn't.

Carnage is everywhere, but beyond the blood and guts and bits of former human spread across the carpet and furniture, the specter of a huge werewolf fills my vision. At least, I assume it's a werewolf. I've never actually seen one that looks like this before; a strange half-form that is neither human nor full wolf. It looks misshapen and wrong, and horror rolls over my skin when it raises its head from where it feasts on a piece of human meat. The eyes gleam with a strange, purple-red glow.

"Ah. Hybrid. You took the bait. You came." The voice is slow and difficult to understand, but the feral expression is unmistakable. "Unlike your sister, you will not escape our reach."

He leaps across the room, so fast I hardly register it.

I don't think there's anything left in me to scream. Not after living the death that took place here only moments earlier. Even though I'm half banshee—a woman renowned for the power in my song—I can't even whimper when a werewolf worse than anything from my wildest nightmares is standing over me, ready to tear out my throat.

This is how I die? The arrogant faerie man was correct, and I didn't listen. Now I'm about to pay the price for my cockiness.

Only...the thing doesn't bite. Instead, its giant maw shoves itself in my face and sniffs greedily. A medallion on a chain around its neck dangles precariously close to my nose. A trail of mucus dribbles off one of his huge yellow teeth and I cringe away to prevent the slobbery wetness from landing on my cheek.

"Delicious......" The breath hisses out as it speaks, delivering with it the stench of blood and something completely rotten. "Give us your name. Your true name."

My stomach heaves. Don't vomit. Don't panic. Don't...

I can't help it. Terror fills me up until there's nothing left but the need to shriek. I was wrong. I do still have a voice. I open my mouth and release all the angst and horror and dread that I've been holding inside since Sienna's death.

The sound is piercing, no longer melodic as I drop all pretence at control of the banshee magic that swirls deep inside.

The thing leaning over me recoils. It's working. He's retreating. But then he's back; the flash of purple in his glaring eyes is stronger.

He grabs me by the arm and jerks me up. "I take you."

That's when I remember the shard of pottery clutched in my fist. I slash with the pointy end of the shard at the furry clawed hand holding me, drawing blood. It drops me, then lurches down and grabs my fist, twisting until I can't help but let go of my piddly little non-weapon.

That defense didn't go as well as I'd hoped.

The creature leans right into my face. My song cuts off as I have to hold my breath to avoid breathing in the stench of rot.

"I want to kill you..." The purple in its vicious eyes flares brighter than the red and it shakes its head repeatedly as if trying to rid itself of something it doesn't like. "I won't. I *won't*. I take her."

My feet aren't working but it doesn't care. It lopes out of the apartment and down the hallway, dragging me along in its wake. I bump along the floor, continuing to scream, and wail, and sob, but there's no one here to save me. My heels scrabble, looking for purchase on the carpet but nothing works. It avoids the elevator and heads straight for the fire stairs.

Oh, God. The creature is going to drag me down six flights of stairs? My back won't survive that. *Where* is it taking me? Why has it not killed me? It wants to. I saw the murderous rage in that terrifying gaze.

Just as we reach the stairwell door a blinding flash of silver light fills the hall.

What the...?

"Unhand her, abomination!"

Tarrien? If I wasn't so utterly terrified in this instant, I'd burst out laughing at his quaint turn of phrase.

I turn my head and confirm that it is, indeed, the faerie man who has come to my assistance. But this version of Tarrien is so different to the other that I can't do anything but gape upward from the floor. There's nothing funny about facing a giant, armor-plated fae warrior with battle fire in his eyes. Especially when he is waving a huge silver sword in one hand and a short but wickedly sharp-looking dagger in the other.

His eyes are as murderous as the monster's, but in Tarrien I welcome the rage. Especially because it is directed at the monster rather than me. I scrabble with my feet, trying to get purchase to stand. When his arm rises as if readying for a blow, I stop scrabbling and go completely limp. The shift in weight throws out the werewolf's balance and it stumbles.

Tarrien slashes sideways with the sword and darts in to plunge the dagger directly into the creature's heart. The latter is unnecessary; the first move sliced the head right off its shoulders. The now-dead headless carcass crashes to the ground beside me. The death-song rushes out of me in a wail filled with angst and grief and I roll on the ground in agony as the pain flows and ebbs and flows again until, finally, the call recedes and silence reigns.

When I come back to myself, I am cradled in Tarrien's arms. He is seated on the ground, my limp body laying across his lap. He rocks me back and forth, crooning in a language I don't recognize. Tendrils of comfort wind around me. I don't want him to stop.

The body of the werewolf is on the floor, half in and half out of the stairwell doorway several meters away. The remains stop the door from closing completely. The head is nowhere to be seen. I think it may have rolled down the stairs.

I shudder at the thought, and Tarrien's arms tighten. Where did the arrogant faerie man go? Who replaced him with this hero who seems to know exactly how to soothe me? I try to smile up at him in thanks, but I'm not sure how successfully the message is communicated.

No sign yet of the police, or anyone else who might have been able to help in time. The neighbors are doing what sensible neighbors do, and steering clear of the horror happening right outside their doors.

"Th...thank you." Unlike my earlier banshee cries, my voice is merely a whisper.

He stops crooning and shifts a lock of hair out of my eyes. "You're back."

"It would appear so." *Though how intact, mentally and physically, remains to be seen.* I shift a little, feeling faintly ridiculous laying across him like this, but for some reason I am unwilling to leave the coziness of his embrace. "Without you, I don't know what would have happened, Tarrien."

"I apologize, Indigo."

I blink. "For what? Saving my life?"

He makes a tsking sound and his brows wrinkle. "Of course not. I apologize for going straight for the kill rather than wounding the creature. I forgot the impact that its death would have on one such as yourself."

I manage a light chuckle. "Never hesitate to go for the kill, Tarrien. Not with a monster like that. I'd rather bear the consequence of the banshee cry than actually die."

My chuckle disappears into nothing as remembered terror fills me.

The sudden tension in my body must be evident because he briefly tightens his hold. "You're safe. I am here to protect you, like I said, and I fully intend to fulfil my duty. Even if you don't want to accept it."

"Well." This time a different kind of tension rushes

through me, one that starts up right about where my left butt cheek is pressed against his groin. It spreads through my system and ends somewhere deep down inside my belly. My heart does that weird flip-flop thing.

"I also apologize for calling you stupid earlier, and making fun of your half-cleaned face. It was rude, considering I barged into your dressing room without warning."

"I...err...don't worry about it. I think saving my life makes us pretty even." I try to use a teasing tone but Tarrien merely nods without smiling.

"That is good. Fae do not enjoy being indebted for longer than they need to."

He doesn't seem to recognize humor or teasing. I grin awkwardly, and then slide out of his embrace and off his lap, though I don't quite have the energy yet to stand.

Tarrien stretches out his legs and leans back against the wall. His sword and dagger have disappeared, as has his impressive dark armor. He's wearing street clothes now—a black tee-shirt and a pair of jeans that are tight enough to showcase the impressive package I inadvertently rubbed against earlier. It's several seconds before I realize I'm staring, and I quickly shift my gaze back up to his.

Laughter lights his silver-gray eyes and a tiny grin lifts the corner of his lips. *Oh.* Seems I was wrong about that. Faerie man does know how to smile. I swallow past the sudden lump in my throat, and look away before the heat in my cheeks has a chance to spread.

The sight of the bloody hallway drains away any semblance of warmth. How could I forget, even for a second?

"Who or what the hell *was* that, Tarrien? I mean, I know it was a—well, I *think* it was a—werewolf?" At his nod, I continue. "But there was something off about it. I mean, more than the misshapen body and the stink. I've met werewolves before, in their human form, at least. Even worked with one once, back in my chorus days—a really charming guy, and a great dancer."

I swallow, remembering tonight's murderous purple rage.

"That creature..." I gesture toward the body without looking at it again. "It wasn't like anything I've ever seen. It was warped. *Wrong.* And why did it only kill that poor person in 602? Why did it not kill me, too? You called it...an *abomination*?"

The serious warrior-face returns. "I do not know the answer as to why it did not kill you, Indigo. But I can confirm that it was, at heart, a supernatural creature turned loup. Crazy. Though it was different to a normal loup, which basically goes mad and kills without reason or discrimination until someone puts it out of its misery."

"A loup?"

"An abomination," he corrects. "A loup that

somehow has retained a modicum of reason. Very concerning. There have been a series of deaths, violent and concentrated in one area—Hatton Grove—in recent months. Plus, other scattered attacks all over the human world, the past several years. Turns out someone is creating these abominations—rogue supernaturals that can reason, and in some cases even work together. Which is almost unheard of. Somehow, someone has learnt how to control these loups, and it appears they are being sent after humans. Some preternaturals—non-humans—are being hurt in the ensuing mess, but primarily, it appears that the target of the violence remains human."

"Hatton Grove? Where's that?"

"It's a small town in a regional area of the state, north-east of this city. Your sister, Aleah, lives there."

"Oh!" I tap my chin, wondering if there's a connection between the attacks. If another of Renna's hybrid children has been at the epicenter of a series of violent occurrences, then maybe the abominations are after banshee hybrids. Maybe the humans being hurt are simply collateral damage.

But why?

From what the monster said after it killed the person in 602, it was deliberately trying to lure me upstairs. And yet, it was going to *take* me, not kill me. Did it murder the other woman because it still needed to fulfil its homicidal instinct?

The random attack that killed my best friend

Sienna a few months ago and left me afraid of being alone for a while, suddenly takes on a whole new meaning.

Oh, God. Was Sienna's death *not* random? At the time, the police said it was just an unfortunate tragedy where my friend happened to be in the wrong place at the wrong time. I always blamed myself because I forgot my purse, and in running back to the theater to get it, I left her alone, providing an opportunity for the attacker to strike. I never considered that it might be more than a random opportunistic attack. Was her death directly because of her association with me? My heart speeds up so fast I feel a little dizzy.

"This is a lot to take in." I close my eyes for a couple of seconds, massaging my temples. "A few hours ago, my life was the same as it always is. I was up on stage, performing..."

Performing the song of death, to dilute the effect when the real thing comes to call. I don't say that last part out loud, but his eyes narrow as if he's aware I cut short my sentence.

"You will need to come back to Faerie with me, Indigo. I can protect you far better there than here. My powers are strongest at home, and as one of Renna's hybrids, it is not safe for you to remain in this realm any longer."

I hold up a hand. "Firstly, please call me Indie. As far as I can remember, the only person who ever called me Indigo was my mother. She also gave me another, ridiculously long name, and told me never to reveal it as it held great power and could be used for evil if it fell into the wrong hands. *So.* Indie will do."

"Indie." He says it slowly, as if savoring the flavor. "I like it."

"Hmm. Well, lucky for me, I do, too. Seeing as it's my name. The second thing is..." *How do I put this nicely*? "There's no way in hell I'm going to leave here and go to Faerie with you, Tarrien. I've heard stories about how time works there. It morphs into weird-as-fuck computations that rarely match what is happening here in the real—I mean, the human—world. Who knows how long I could be stuck there? I could hang out with you for a day, and arrive back here to find half a lifetime has passed. I have a life, there are people I care about, a *cat*—"

"You could bring your cat. I *think*."

"You *think*? Yeah, sorry, it's not going to—"

The door to the stairwell flings fully open at the same time as the elevator pings and opens. A swarm of masked and uniformed figures pile into the hallway from every direction.

olice. Not ordinary cops, either, by the look of the logo on their protective gear and weaponry. These cops are from the supernatural division of the Australian Federal Police. SUDAP.

The ones who came up the stairs trip over the body of the werewolf, and all hell breaks loose around Tarrien and I with yelling, flailing arms and legs, and an altogether chaotic scene.

After a moment in which I wait for them to point their guns in our faces, I realize they haven't noticed us. How is that possible? Are they blind?

A pair of suited-up cops rushes past us to the door of apartment 602, without even glancing our way. I start to clamber to my feet but Tarrien grabs my upper arm.

"Don't move, banshee. I've thrown a protective

bubble around us, but it'll burst if you move too quickly."

"A bubble? Like a cloak of magic? We're invisible then? Like, really invisible?"

The concept is exciting when read about in books or seen in movies, but the reality is kind of strange. They are so close I could reach out and touch them. I would probably give them the fright of their lives if I did so.

One of the cops pauses in front of us. It's a female and, surprisingly, she looks familiar. She frowns and squats in front of me, running one hand over the carpet as if searching for a clue, before lifting her head and staring straight at me. The long fingers of her left hand twitch on the gun in her grip.

I try for normal. "Um...hi?"

She doesn't answer.

Instead, Tarrien says quietly, "She can't hear you, Indie. But I think she can sense the bubble. I don't know how. There's something about her...she's fae, or part at least..." His face shows sudden strain, as if he's finding it difficult to hold the magic in place under the strength of her regard. "You look a little like twins."

My heart jumps. *Is she...banshee?*

The woman reaches out, her fingers almost grazing my hair as they explore the air between us, and I stare deep into her caramel-flecked green eyes wondering how it is possible that we can be this close without her seeing me. The eyes are familiar. *My* eyes? They are more hazel than my green ones, and her long dark hair is drawn back into a plait rather than hanging loose like mine. And yet, it really does feel like I'm staring into a mirror.

Those features are harder than mine, though. Hard, and cynical and uncompromising. Despite my surface bravado, I suspect I don't have half the inner toughness of this woman squatting in front of me.

What the actual heck? Who is she? Are we related?

A voice down the hallway calls out and snags the woman's attention. "Maewen. Over here. Another one of those medallion things."

The moment of almost-connection is lost as she jumps to her feet and rushes away. Tarrien visibly slumps at her departure, before straightening his shoulders. "Another minute and she'd have breached the bubble. Don't suppose you have a sister named Maewen, do you?"

Another of Renna's banshee hybrids? Those eyes... I glance down the hallway, knowing in my heart that I've just stared into the face of one of my half-sisters, but the woman has disappeared into the blood-and-gore-filled apartment. If she's part-banshee, how can she bear to do a job like that? Even a cop with a desk job would be exposed to death on occasion, and this woman looks like the last person who would suffer the boredom of a desk job.

If she is a human-fae hybrid, and one of Renna's children, how the hell can she tolerate working as a cop? How does she deal with that level of horror every day? Violence and death smell, and they hurt, and they almost tear a banshee's insides to shreds. If she's a cop it must be part of her job, I guess, but if her job involves death, how does she function with any semblance of normality?

Sudden exhaustion fills me. "No idea. Can we please leave, Tarrien? I want to get away from the stench of death."

The thought of the mess down the hallway is making me sick to the stomach, even though I've been studiously avoiding looking at it.

Was that really my sister, or at least, one of my half-sisters? I know I have several, out there somewhere, though I've never tried to seek out any of them. Nor has anyone sought for me—at least to my knowledge.

I'm lost in thought about the female cop when Tarrien touches my forearm. A spark of energy sizzles through me and he removes his fingers.

What *is* this physical connection between us?

"When I say *now*, I want you to stand very slowly, Indie, keeping pace with me, and then take hold of my hand. I will maintain the bubble around us as long as I can, but I'll have to drop it right before I transport us out of here."

"Can we go home, please?"

"Yes, of course. I'll take you to Faer—"

Not this again. I almost growl in frustration. "*My* home. One level down in this building. Please."

His eyes narrow but then he nods. "All right."

Together we rise slowly, as if perfectly synchronized, and then he reaches out. I slip my hand into his, entwining our fingers, and that previously felt energy spark flares once again between us. Before I can react to the zing, he has already laid his other hand over mine.

"Ready. *Now*." I'm blinded by a flash of silver light.

A shout from the hallway indicates we've finally been seen, but then we're away, and it matters not. The light swallows us up and I can't see a thing. I feel all stretched and kind of hollow, like someone is pushing me through a tight space, and then the squeezing pressure eases and the light recedes and I find myself standing with Tarrien next to my bed.

My bed? *Really? That's a very specific destination.*

He drops my hand and turns to survey the room before a slow smile transforms his face from severe to handsome. My heart skips a beat. *Wow*. He really should smile more often.

"I tapped into your thoughts to guide us," he says. "Interesting that it led...*here*."

Oh. Heat infuses my cheeks. So, I can't exactly blame *his* magic for leading us to my bed.

I clear my throat. "What now, Tarrien? I need more information about all of this, to understand what's going on and how we might be able to stop it happening again."

But first, I need a shower. I don't say those words

aloud but I don't need to. Both of us are covered in blood and there's a dreadful smell that has followed us here, even though we're now on a different floor of the building than the carnage remaining on level six.

"Take a shower, Indie, and then I will follow suit if you allow. I don't wish to stain your home with anything tainted by violence."

"Of course, you can shower after me." Given the fact that I've only just met the guy tonight, I should be afraid to step into the bathroom and get naked with him hanging out in the next room, but part of me is comforted by his presence.

There's no denying that I was in a world of trouble before Tarrien arrived. Even though that monstrous creature clearly wanted to take me somewhere rather than kill me on the spot, I doubt I would have survived being dragged on my back down several flights of stairs. At the very least, it would have resulted in some broken bones. Maybe even a broken neck.

With Tarrien keeping an eye out, I will be able to scrub myself clean for as long as I wish, and not worry about what other monster might be creeping in to the apartment while I'm under the stream of cleansing water.

"You saved my life tonight," I remind him. "The very least I can offer you is a hot shower."

"I'll stand here until you finish. That way I won't get any of this mess on your furniture."

"Um, probably best if you stand out there, if you

don't mind." I point toward the lounge room. Safer for my own piece of mind to have him away from my bed, especially if I'm about to get naked.

I duck my head as I scurry into the bathroom, so he can't read anything more into my words. Images of a wet and very bare fae warrior soaping up his body begin to fill my head. Oh, God. I really hope he doesn't have mind-reading power.

I remove my ruined pajamas and throw them into the plastic bag-lined trash can, before scrubbing off the remaining gore and horror from my hair and body in the hottest shower I can stand.

How will Tarrien fit in my tiny little shower cubicle? I have a one-bedroom city-style apartment here in East Melbourne, and space is at a premium. The small bathroom suits me just fine, but a large man like Tarrien will struggle to fit. Once again, the thought of his tall, muscled and very *naked* body arouses feelings I can't afford to experience.

Why do I keep thinking about Tarrien in a sexual way? Too much has happened tonight to even entertain the idea of sex with a very handsome stranger, let alone act on those thoughts. Tonight's events, layered on top of what happened to my friend a few months ago, should have me running as far and as fast as I can away from anyone connected to the supernatural world.

Instead, I can't stop imagining what it would be like to sink myself onto the sexy hard flesh of the fae warrior in the next room, and ride him until my body and my senses are finally sated.

When I'm finished with my shower, the citrus flavor of my body wash mixes with the musky scent from my shampoo, filling the room with a familiar and pleasant perfume. I dress in an old tee-shirt and fleecy trackpants—as far from sexy as I can find in my cupboard—and head out to the lounge area to hand my fae guest a clean towel and let him have his turn.

True to his word, he is still standing where I directed him, in the middle of the room. Lola is back in her usual spot on the couch, which surprises me. Normally when strangers visit, she hides in the tiniest spot she can find, all curled up in a tight ball in my bedroom cupboard as if that will reduce the chance of someone actually discovering her.

Instead, she's stretched out on the end seat on her back, with her stomach exposed, as if without a care in the world. She doesn't even shift from that position when Tarrien heads off to the bathroom.

I busy myself tidying up a little, washing the dishes from my earlier supper and hoping for distraction from my thoughts. Eventually I reach a state of calm... until Tarrien re-emerges, wrapped in nothing but the towel I handed him earlier. A towel that is clearly way too small for such a large and impressively muscled man as this fae.

His barely covered package is so prominent it practically hits me in the face. Well, not really, but for some reason—yet again—I can't seem to take my eyes off of it. *What is wrong with me?*

Unlike Lola, who settles further into lethargy with a rasping purr, my body shifts into overdrive. Heat rushes through me as thoughts of running my hands over every inch of his body fill my head. His chest is hairless and firm, the stomach wash-board flat and rippling with the best set of abs I've ever laid eyes on. His skin is pale, unlike the usual tan that denotes fashion here in Australia, but the smooth creaminess of that expanse of chest decorated by two perfectly rounded dark nipples, calls to my body with an intensity no man has ever managed to create within me, before this moment.

My fingers curl into my palms in an attempt to stop myself reaching out to caress him.

Despite my stage persona being centered around oozing sexuality, I'm not actually too experienced myself in that regard. I can count on one hand the number of lovers I've actually had over the years, though I have definitely seen my share of impressive abs in the showbusiness industry. Many of those abs belong to men who prefer other men, which means I could look and joke comfortably with them, as they joked back with me in a safe way. A way that meant nothing other than a bit of simple theater-buddy camaraderie.

Nothing about Tarrien is safe. At least, that's how I feel when I look at him. He seems completely unaware that every single inch of him calls to my woman bits in a way that is difficult to ignore.

What is it about him that causes this effect? Is it because he's fae? Or is it just *him*, sexy as fuck and not even really aware of it? I think that latter fact is one of the things that makes him seem sexier than anyone I've ever known. The males in the industry in which I work—straight or gay—are fully aware of their effect on the people around them.

My breasts are achy and full, and my nipples harden as I imagine smooshing them against all that delectable hard muscle and silken skin.

I seriously hope his magic does not extend to reading lascivious thoughts, or if it does, that he has the decency to not delve too deep into my head. I risk a glance up at his face and realize his cheeks are as ruddy as mine feel. Is that because of *my* thoughts, or are his own heading in the same direction?

"Can you read minds?"

His brows slide upward.

"No." After a moment, he clears his throat. "Can you?"

When I shake my head, he seems to relax a touch, and focuses his gaze somewhere over my shoulder. "I think perhaps I should dress, and then we can talk."

"Good idea. Wait. I...don't have any male clothing here."

"That's not an issue. I will return to my own apartment here in the city to fetch some."

"You live here? I thought…"

"I live in Faerie, but I do keep an apartment in the human realm. It moves around with me, depending on where I am based at the time."

"Oh. Sure." An apartment that moves around? A lot has happened tonight, so I'm not sure why that fact in particular seems so hard for my brain to process.

Tarrien shrugs. "It will take only an instant. I will be back shortly." He gestures to the ring that still decorates his thumb. "Fae magic infuses this. Handy little thing. Good for communication and travel."

Wait. Was that an attempt at a joke? He disappears before I can read his features properly.

I flop onto the couch next to Lola. "Holy crap, girl. I need to get myself back under control before he returns."

Lola groans and shifts, then resettles into her seemingly comatose state.

"Mmm. Thanks for the support, Lols."

At least if he puts some clothing back on, we might be able to focus on the important stuff. *You're focusing on the important stuff right now*, my mind teases. I lean my head against the back of the sofa, annoyed with my body's response to Tarrien, and try some slow deep breathing. *Calm. Calm.* My mini-meditation doesn't work. When I can't get him out of my thoughts, I move instead to the kitchen area and busy myself making a hot drink before returning to the lounge.

This time, when Tarrien pops back in, he is fully

clothed, though the tightness of his fresh tee-shirt and jeans does not do much to hide the impressive physique. Especially not now that I've practically seen it all and know what's hidden underneath.

"I've made tea." My tone is breathless, and I clear my throat. "Peppermint and standard. Do you drink it? Or would you prefer coffee?"

I indicate the tray on the coffee table as he takes a seat beside me. *Hmm. This couch is very crowded with the three of us squished in together like this.*

Silently, I will Lola to move so I can slide across. She raises her head briefly and blinks at me, then lays her head down again, ignoring my wordless plea.

"Peppermint, yes," Tarrien says. "It will remind me of home. Thank you."

He proceeds to pour and then sip from a fragile china cup, which he cradles in two large hands with surprising delicacy.

God. How can he even make sipping tea look sensual?

The only way to distract myself from the sexiness on my couch, is to focus back on the reason he's here in the first place.

"Okay, Tarrien, time to talk. *What* is going on, and what the hell are we going to do about it?"

Chapter Four

TARRIEN

When Indie stares at me with those amazing emerald eyes, I lose my train of thought. Why can I not stop fantasizing about ripping off her tee-shirt and those horrible track pants? The fact that she must have purposefully grabbed the most shapeless things from her closet does not hide the sexy curves of her body, nor the deliciously smooth pale skin on her neck that cries out to be kissed. Even her feet, bare and ruby-tipped with those perfectly manicured nails, scream sexy.

Control. I need to regain control of my runaway body, before it gets both of us into trouble. Remember your duties as a winter warrior.

My mind eventually finds its way back to consider her question. She wants to know what is going on, and what to do about it.

Just as I open my mouth to answer, the tip of her

tongue darts out and moistens her lips and I lose focus once again. The heat of desire swells my loins and I shift uncomfortably, wondering if she knows the effect her proximity has on me. Why does this hybrid cause my brain to switch off and my cock to charge up to the ready as if plugged into an imaginary electrical socket?

If I were vampire—one of those descended from the blood of Dracule—I could perhaps understand it. The scent of hybrid fae is as delicious to a vamp as a drug of addiction. But I'm *fae*, not vampire. She's half-human, half-fae. Her scent shouldn't send every nerve ending in my body into raptures. Her delectable, exotic, slightly citrus scent that fills my nostrils and chases coherent thought away.

I release an involuntary groan.

"Tarrien." Her voice whispers across my skin with the power of a true banshee. She might be only half-and-half, but this woman knows how to wield her influence. It is not so surprising, I guess, given how many years she must have trained for her role on stage. A trained singer, who holds the power of a banshee in her heart?

My breath huffs out shakily. How can I resist such a combination?

I lean in toward her. "You smell like home. Everything I love about home."

Did those words just come out of my mouth? I sound ridiculous. Do I even care, though, when I am about to claim her as mine? I reach my fingers into her hair and clutch her head, steadying her to be ready for my onslaught.

"Home, *here*?" she whispers.

"No. Faerie."

Something deep in her expression flickers. Something wounded and afraid. I hold myself motionless instead of going in for the kiss. She is trying hard not to show it, whatever *it* is, but there is more going on here than Indie is letting on.

"I intend to kiss you, Indie. But I won't, if you do not wish it."

She hesitates, worrying at her bottom lip with perfect white teeth. Just as I am about to release a disappointed sigh and pull away, she darts in and kisses me full on the mouth.

I forget everything but the feel of her lips on mine. Soft and sweet and yet demanding, all at once. Even though it was my intention to kiss her, the bold move takes me aback and it is several moments before I return the kiss.

When I do, it is as if everything around us disappears and we are the only two in the universe. I part her lips and taste her mouth, exploring her with my mouth and tongue, and allowing her to explore me in return. She tastes both sweet and enticing. Like her scent, there is a hint of citrus on her lips, underlaid with a sexy musk flavor that I sense is completely her own.

She releases a tiny moan that vibrates in her throat

and carries upward until it enters me. The sound is so enticing it drags an answering groan from deep within me.

Her essence surrounds me. I am drowning in it. I cannot get enough.

Eventually, with apparent reluctance, she pulls back and away.

"That was...unexpected." Her voice is breathless, her lips lush and full from our intense and prolonged connection. She touches a hand to her throat as if trying to contain the frantic beat of her heart. She can't hide it. I can see its wild tattoo—the frenetic beat matching my own—until her other hand flutters up and over her throat too. The effect of our kiss on her pulse rate disappears from my view.

I push a stray lock of hair off her face, my fingers itching to explore more of her body.

"Unexpected and delightful. I am not overly familiar with...*this*, Indie." I capture one of her hands and move it down to hover above my groin. "It is not often a winter warrior's path in life to enjoy the fruits of the physical."

Her fingers spasm in mine, the movement bringing her into contact, ever-so-lightly, with my burgeoning flesh. My breath hitches in my throat before I can control the response, and her eyes, when she raises her gaze to mine, are wide and a little confused.

"Please tell me you're not a virgin, Tarrien."

My cheeks heat. How is it that this woman creates heat everywhere, all the way from my cock to my face?

"Of *course* not. I have had many women, over the years, but I am four hundred and twenty-three years old, so the word *many* does not necessarily mean *frequent*."

I cannot believe I am having this discussion. There are far more important things to talk about than my sexual prowess, or lack thereof.

Her beautiful wide mouth quirks in a grin. "Good. I don't think I could cope with a virgin warrior. Nor a promiscuous one. Sounds like you have just the right amount of innocence and experience."

Before I realize what is happening, her hand slips out of mine and cradles my cock in a clear invitation for more. The warmth of her touch leaches through my jeans and a strange noise escapes me before I can stifle it. Not quite a groan and not quite a growl; somewhere halfway between.

"Do not do that, banshee, unless you truly want it."

"I do want it. I *need* it." Her tone is fierce, and again I get the impression there is something she is leaving unsaid, but when her fingers spasm again I lose what little thought process I have left and lunge for her, crushing her body beneath mine and capturing her lips in another passionate kiss. This time, I am determined the kiss will be mine to claim, not the other way around.

Energy sizzles along every nerve path in my body

and I groan again, deep down in my throat. She moans in return, a tiny sound that enters my body through our kiss, in a rush of sweet breath. The sound is all the more sensual for its quietness. Her tongue dances with mine and our lips move into a rhythm that directs all the blood in my body down into my groin. The heavy ache is almost unbearable. Lust is not supposed to feel as intense as this, is it? All heat and agony and ecstasy.

How can I possibly resist the lure of Indie's warmth?

When at last we break apart, my breath rattles harshly in my throat. It is as if being near her has sucked all the air out of the room. I need more, so much more, than this. I need everything Indie has to give.

"I'm a winter warrior, sworn to maintain distance." It is a token effort at resistance. We both know I don't really mean it.

"Hmm," she says playfully. "Then I'll just have to melt that ice around your heart, won't I?"

"I think you already have."

I don't care that I might compromise my duty. Not in this moment. I only care that she, too, is panting hard, her flutters of breath puffing out with every rasping exhale. I love that her state of excitement is solely due to *me*. I love that she seems to be as affected by our proximity as I am.

"I don't know why, but I'm desperate to have sex

with you." Her voice is both puzzled and erotic, tempting in a way I never expected.

I cannot believe this beautiful, warm, passionate creature is Lady Renna's daughter. The two could not be more different. I shuck that thought out of my head. I do not wish to think of that woman while this exotic beauty is offering herself to me like this.

"And I with you," I respond, before either of us changes our mind. "It is not a good idea; I suspect we both know that. And yet I cannot seem to concentrate on anything but the thought of sinking my hardness into your warm, sweet body and taking you to the heights of pleasure and beyond. I want to make love with you, Indie."

She smiles then, and stands up, holding out her hand for me to take.

"I love the quaint way you talk. Come into the bedroom, Tarrien. Let's make love. That sounds so much nicer than simply having sex."

My heart jumps, and kicks up the pace ten-fold. I take her proffered hand and allow her to lead me back into the bedroom. Her king-size bed dwarfs the tiny space, but I am not expecting to spend much time on the floor. She turns and faces me, and drops my hand so she can shuck off her old tee-shirt. Her naked breasts are as full and as spectacular as their sensual promise in her tight red dress when she was up on that stage, and my already-firm cock hardens even more.

Her gaze drifts downward and a seductive grin hovers about her lips.

"You've risen to the occasion very impressively." Slowly, she starts to lower her tracksuit pants, wriggling her hips from side to side in a sensual striptease that takes far too much time to complete.

I arch a brow.

"I have a better technique than that," I tease, and wave my hand. The remainder of her clothing, and mine, disappear into the ether. "That's better. Don't you think?"

The look of shock on her face lends an edge of joy to the situation.

"Well," she says. "Well. That's not a bad technique at all."

We stand face to face, completely naked. She is utterly beautiful, all curves and pale skin and luscious long legs. Her mound is bare and I cannot take my eyes from it. That is, until she shifts backward and sits on the edge of the bed. The movement brings her breasts back into my focus.

A waft of her delicious scent floats over me and I inhale deeply, enjoying the way it makes me feel decadent and carefree.

My spirits lift. Carefree is not a state to which I am frequently accustomed. And it feels damn good.

I advance toward Indie and she lays down and raises her arms above her head. The action ensures I have an uninterrupted view of those beautiful breasts.

Their rosy peaks are hard and pointing upward. I can't wait to taste her flesh.

Then her legs drop, one to each side, opening up that perfect mound to fully expose the pink lips of her pussy, her swollen bud and the entrance to her channel. The sight almost brings me to climax, right there in front of her.

"By the gods, you are so incredibly sexy, Indie." My voice is hoarse, but for once I do not care whether or not she can see the extent of her effect on me. I love that almost choked-up sensation that closes my throat as I imagine seating my ready flesh at her channel entrance and thrusting hard and deep within the tight embrace of her body.

But first, I have to taste her.

I kneel by the bed and she pushes her hips up toward me. I bend my head and connect with her pussy lips in the most intimate kiss in the world, sucking her bud into my mouth and swirling my tongue around it. I have never tasted anything more divine. I slide my tongue down her slit to find her channel entrance, dipping my tongue briefly inside her hot body and then out again, loving the slick wetness and the heat. She bucks beneath my mouth, moaning and gasping, and I return to attend her clitoris again, working it hard while I slide a finger gently inside her body.

She is as tight and wet as I imagined. I cannot wait to seat myself properly inside her.

Her bucking and writhing increases in tempo and around my finger I feel the tell-tale tightening and clenching of muscle wall as she nears climax. My own body is fighting hard to maintain control. There is no ice left whatsoever around my heart in the melting pot of warmth that surrounds us. The heat in my groin is a furnace begging for release.

She begins to spasm as an orgasm takes her, and cries out in a guttural shriek as her channel clutches and releases around my thrusting finger. Her body shudders beneath me.

I climb up onto the bed and balance over her on my hands and knees, staring down into her eyes. They are half-closed in the aftermath of her release, and yet still the brilliant emerald color peeks out from beneath her lowered lashes. No hazel left. Passion has burned it all away and left the brilliance of a precious stone in its wake.

"I have never wanted anyone as much as I want you right this instant." I bend my elbows and take one of her perfect breasts into my mouth, suckling on the puckered nipple until a tiny cry releases from her mouth.

"Oh yes, Tarrien. That feels so good. *So* good!"

I cross to her other breast and suckle some more, pinching the first nipple between my thumb and forefinger and twirling the nub as I lick and suck at the other one.

She reignites beneath me, moving more

languorously this time round, and I lower my hips until the head of my organ grazes her clitoris. She arches up and into me, the action firming the connection and drawing a gasp from my own throat. She feels so warm and slick. Another of her hip thrusts ensues, and I can't contain the groan that erupts.

"Gods, Indie. I want to be inside you so badly."

"What are you waiting for, then?" Her breathing is harsh and uneven. Encouraged by another nudge upward with her hips, I slide my organ down her slit, enjoying the heat and the slick wetness, until I am exactly where I want to be, right at the entrance to her body.

I drive hard, sliding into her in one quick movement. It is as if our bodies are made for one another; we fit so well. Her pussy lips and the muscles deep within her channel grab tight. Her legs wrap around my buttocks and hold me fast. I bend and capture her mouth in a brief but passionate kiss, wondering if she enjoys the taste of herself on my lips, and then I cannot wait any longer. I begin to thrust in earnest.

She matches my rhythm and we gain momentum, escalating quickly in the age-old dance of love. Her moans mingle with mine, until finally, I feel her tense even further, holding perfectly still for a second or two as if poised on the edge of a precipice. Then she tumbles over into a second orgasm. Her body arches beneath me and she begins to shudder and tremble. A scream releases from her, muffled against my shoulder.

The sound tips me over the edge, too, and an unintelligible roar bursts from my throat as I release my seed in a rush. Heat and wetness, and a deep sense of connectedness in that moment, warms me right to my core.

I collapse against her, spent, and then roll us onto our sides, wanting to remain seated deep inside her but not wanting my weight to crush her.

Perspiration coats my skin, and hers. It takes several seconds before my breathing even attempts to return to normal.

She grins at me, sleepily, and reaches up a hand to caress my cheek. "That was pretty damn good, faerie man."

So much for ice. This woman has melted everything within a ten-foot radius of my heart.

I turn my head into her caress and manage to land a gentle kiss on her palm. "It *was* pretty damn good, little banshee."

We lay in sated silence. On my part I am content just to hold her, and from the way she curls her warm body into mine and then settles with a sigh, I believe she feels the same sense of peace.

I wonder at the joy of feeling heat both within my body, and outside it. When I have had sex in the past, it has always been an act that takes place in the moment. An act that is over as quickly as it starts. Solstice festivals in Faerie—when many of the Winter Court's inhabitants gather to celebrate the change of season—are highly conducive to sex, but rarely to intimacy.

This—lying here with Indie wrapped in my arms—feels like intimacy. Against my usually wintery form, her curves feel good. They feel just right, in fact. I tighten my embrace around her and she shifts within my arms and gazes up at me. Surprisingly, her expression turns serious and reflects a hint of sadness.

I raise myself up on one elbow. "What is it? Did you not...enjoy...I thought...?"

Confusion rushes through me. Was I so caught up in my own need for Indie that I did something wrong? Admittedly I am not hugely experienced in the ways of the flesh, but I thought it went rather well. Did she not attain as much pleasure from it as me?

"Of course, I enjoyed it, Tarrien. Could you not tell? Two orgasms in the space of a few minutes..." She grins at me, but it doesn't reach her eyes.

"You still seem sad. What is it?"

Even as I ask the question, everything that happened earlier rushes back into my mind. Of *course*, she must be upset. How could I have forgotten the attack?

As a fae warrior, I am trained in battle and even expect it, at times. Indie, on the other hand, is a theatre performer well entrenched in the human world. In fact, she seems to have embraced her human half as much as it is possible to do so, while carrying banshee blood. What occurred tonight would have been so foreign to her it is actually a miracle she was able to put it aside at all.

"That was insensitive," I say. "Given what happened earlier."

"It's not that. Well, I guess it is, but not how you probably think. It's just me, overthinking things. I have a tendency to do that sometimes," she says. "But I was lying here wondering, is it death, do you think, that led us to do this? To have sex when we hardly know one another and have just been through something really...horrific."

She shudders, still tight in my arms.

"I was certainly not thinking about death when we...err..." I don't quite know how to answer her. I was not expecting a question like that.

"I'm sorry, you probably think I'm nuts. Of course, I wasn't thinking about it, either. What we just did was wonderful, Tarrien. But death and dying is a big part of my existence, whether I like it or not. Actually, I hate it."

Pity for her plight rises in my chest. I suppose I never really considered what it might be like to be a banshee. Even a half-banshee.

Her eyes flash, as if she senses my pity band doesn't want to accept it. "Experiencing the end, over and over again, is unfortunately my 'normal'. Sex with you was definitely not what I intended when I asked you to bring me back home, Tarrien, but for some reason I needed it. Desperately. And I felt like it was especially *because* of what happened earlier, not in spite of it. Does that seem warped to you?"

"No. It makes a strange kind of sense, actually. As long as you don't regret..."

"I don't."

I relax back against the pillow and stroke her face. "Do you think perhaps it is because sex is aimed toward life? Even..."

"Even though I'm a banshee hybrid and as such, cannot create life within my own body?"

Shock courses through me at her stiffly delivered words.

"No," I say. "That is not what I was going to say."

"Oh." She rolls onto her back and stares at the ceiling. "I might be a bit over-sensitive about that fact. So, what were you going to say?"

"I was just going to say, even when it is just sex for pleasure's sake, and not specifically for procreation. It definitely felt...well, life-giving in a way. Hot and warm and good. Though I hope I haven't damaged my ability to protect and heal. I went against everything a winter warrior stands for, to couple with you."

She flinches and then frowns, still staring at the ceiling and not at me, and I realize too late it is not the correct thing to have said. When it comes to Indie, I don't ever seem able to get it right. She rolls slowly and deliberately away and out of my embrace, before sitting up and crossing her arms over her chest. The only disadvantage of a king-size bed is that there is room to separate fully, if one or both parties wish it.

I want to reach across the vast expanse between us and pull her back into my arms. But somehow, I seem to have hurt her feelings, even though I speak only the truth.

I try to explain more fully. "My father was a winter warrior, a long time ago. He gave in to the call of passion, and was banished from Faerie by King Tryppton for his misbehavior, along with his lover, Rhiannon. Queen of the Winter Court."

"Jesus!"

"Yes." I nod vigorously, glad that she seems to understand the depth of such a transgression. "So, you get it, then. What you and I just did was delightful, but it is not healthy, and it cannot happen again. I cannot risk diluting my powers. Not when I need them most."

If I have sex with you, I risk not being able to protect you. I don't verbalize that last thought, but I am certain she now understands.

Her mouth forms a thin line before she speaks. "Heaven forbid that sex with me would damage what you most hold dear. Yes, we must definitely never let it happen again, winter warrior. I think it's time for you to leave."

"Wait...but—"

"Now. I really want you to leave now."

"I don't understand."

She turns away, presenting me with her back. Her

naked back is as delectable as the front view. My loins tighten, despite the fact that my desire was sated only a short time earlier.

"That's the problem, Tarrien," she says. "Get out of my bed. And please get out of my house."

Icicles instantly reform around my heart. I guess that answers the question about whether or not I caused permanent damage. Seems the heat was only temporary.

The look on Indie's face as she finally half-turns and glares at me over her shoulder says I have overstayed my welcome. She raises a brow, as if waiting for me to comply with her demand.

"Fine." I jump out of bed and dress quickly, ignoring her covert yet angry glances at my body. At least, I try to ignore them. It is as if she still wants me, but hates herself for the weakness. "I will return, banshee. This threat is only going to get bigger, and I am bound to protect you, whether either of us want that, or not."

I touch my filigree ring and step toward the circle of silver mist that will take me out of this realm. Just before I leave, I turn back for one last look at Indigo, unsure what caused the sudden rift between us. Was it something I said? Does she think I regret what happened between us? I was so concerned that she might have regretted our act, that I didn't consider she might be wondering the same. I wish I was more skilled in the ways of dealing with women and sexual relationships.

I open my mouth to say something—anything—but her green eyes shoot daggers and she shakes her head, just the once, before jumping up and running into her bathroom.

I close my mouth without speaking further and move into the mist. We didn't talk properly about the risk to Indie's life posed by the abominations, but we will. I am determined to return soon to ensure I fulfill my promise to Indie's mother. Not for Renna's sake, anymore, but for Indie.

Despite the fact that my relationship with the sexy banshee songstress has just turned as cold as my Winter Court home in Faerie, I will not allow her to succumb to the growing threat. I don't know how I will keep her safe, but somehow, I have to. The alternative is unthinkable.

Chapter Five

INDIGO

Is he really that dumb? Can any man—fae or human—seriously not know how offensive those words are? I cannot believe I let him into my bed. Of all the men—or women—I could choose to have sex with to briefly forget the call of the banshee, I can't believe I chose a fae man so severely lacking in people skills.

I know that I'm being ridiculously over-sensitive, but it's been a long while since I took a lover and the timing of it seemed to ram home the fact that my life centers squarely around death. To have that sensitivity compounded by Tarrien instantly telling me afterward that he thinks it unhealthy to be with me...

"Grr." I stare at my reflection, as angry with myself as I am with him for giving in to lust, noting the marks on my body from Tarrien's lips and mouth and fingers. An ache deep down in my belly immediately starts up as I remember what it felt like to have him moving deep inside me.

Stop thinking about that. He doesn't want any more of it. He just wants to protect you, not ravish you.

Gradually, the need subsides and I re-enter the bedroom once I'm sure he's gone. *God damn it.* I didn't even get to find out more about what is going on with those foul loup creatures.

I curl into a ball on the bed and hug my belly. My inability to have children has never bothered me before. It still doesn't bother me now. Maybe it has something to do with the fact that I grew up in foster care and never had the chance to dream about having children or a family of my own, or maybe it's simply innate, but for whatever reason, I'm not really into kids.

I've never met anyone who made me wonder what it would be like to have young ones running around to complete the family.

Until Tarrien. Maybe that was why I immediately assumed he was referencing that, when in fact, he was already in damage control mode in relation to his damn stupid iced-up heart.

"Idiot."

Lola strolls into the bedroom and sits on the carpet staring up at me, blinking slowly as if asking who I'm calling an idiot.

"*He's* an idiot. A bloody big one," I tell the cat.

She blinks once more, and then begins to wash her face.

"*I'm* a goddamn idiot, too."

Lola stops mid-lick and stares at me with all the disdain a cat can manifest and then turns and stalks out of the room. Yep. She agrees with me.

Why can't I stop thinking about how sexy he is, despite his obviously insensitive nature? And why did I send him away, without finding out more about what the hell is going on with the loups and the threat toward humans?

What did he mean about the threat only going to get bigger? What exactly *is* the threat, and why does he still need to protect me? Are there many more of those loup creatures out there?

The image of the person upstairs in 602 pops back into my head, despite my best efforts to block out the carnage. A sick feeling fills my gut at the knowledge that it was most likely my presence in the building that contributed to the poor woman's death.

Bait, the creature said, before he died. *I took their bait.* That means it is unlikely to be a coincidence that the victim happened to live directly above me, and her dying drew me out like a moth to a flame. They deliberately killed someone, just to draw me out.

An innocent casualty in a war I didn't even know was being waged. My thoughts head straight back to Sienna. *Oh, my dear friend. Were you also bait?*

I hate death. I hate it with a passion. And both the

neighbor's death upstairs, and my best friend's a few months ago, were hideous and violent, full of pain and terror. I wish I never had to experience anything like that ever again.

But unfortunately, I know I will.

I experience all of them, at least those within a certain range. I've never really tested the limit of the range, and that isn't exactly something I want to do. But at a guess, I would say within a mile or so, perhaps just under.

If something happens outside that range, I might feel a twinge of unease, perhaps a tweak of pain and sadness, or sometimes even the strange lethargy that afflicted me at the theater, but nothing more.

The banshee magic that swirls inside of me is one of the key reasons I chose to become a singer. When I was young, death almost crippled me, every time it arrived. The force was so uncontrolled and wild, that I lived in a state of dread for years, until the day one of my foster parents—the only one who ever showed me any level of genuine caring—suggested I might be able to channel some of my distress into song.

That foster parent was the only person in the first sixteen years of my life who took the time to help me. She even paid for a course of singing lessons, and for that I will be forever grateful. Those lessons led to small parts in musicals, then working in the theater chorus for several years, to finally being the star act in a show centered around my voice. Being on stage and singing in such a controlled manner does help—at least a little—to curb some of the banshee angst.

I can channel all the terror and fear and everything negative that comes with being part-banshee, into my voice, so that it becomes a pressure release and allows me to survive those moments when the death call arrives. Not enough to stop it altogether, but I visualize it as being similar to a valve that releases a tiny bit of steam at a time.

Singing for pleasure instead of pain seems so much healthier than writhing around on the floor wondering if this is the moment the magic becomes too much, and *I'm* finally going to end up dead, too.

THE CABARET CLUB is full when I arrive with Dreya. I can't believe she talked me into this but the show after-party, held at the intimate club across the street from our much larger theater, is actually being thrown in my honor. It was my ten-year anniversary with the company last week, and my fifth year as lead performer.

All members of the troupe, as well as several of our company patrons, and even a few of my regular audience members, have been invited as guests to help celebrate the milestone. It is also a good opportunity for our marketing team to promote some of the upcoming shows—or so I've been told. There will apparently be a team of photographers and PR people on hand to document the evening. I guess it would be churlish to not at least make a brief appearance.

I hate show after-parties, generally, and avoid them as much as I can, but since Tarrien stomped out of my bedroom and popped away in a flash of silver light several days ago, I have to admit, I've been moping around a bit. Maybe tonight will give me something to think about other than a particularly sexy and extremely annoying faerie man.

"You've been a proper wet blanket this week," Dreya says. "I hope you snap out of it soon. It's getting annoying."

"I know," I reply.

She's not being rude. We have the kind of relationship where truth is valued, and Dreya is never afraid to tell it like she sees it. In this case, she's absolutely correct. I haven't been myself since the night my upstairs neighbor died and I tried to block out the angst by losing myself in Tarrien's arms. It's not like me to sulk as long as this.

"I'm sorry, Dreya. I'll try and be a bit more fun from now on."

"Good! Now, don't forget," she says, snagging two sparkling wines from a passing waiter and shoving one of them into my hand, "you have to make a speech thanking everyone for coming along to celebrate your anniversary."

"Oh, hell!" I forgot about that part.

"Drink up, and remember! *Fun!* You need to let loose and smile a bit more. You might even meet someone sexy if you do that." Dreya flashes me a cheeky grin. "Someone as sexy as that faerie guy. Though he did set the bar pretty high."

She winks and disappears into the crowd.

I stare around, knowing most of those in attendance already and positive I won't meet anyone remotely as sexy as Tarrien. I remind myself I can appreciate the warrior's sexiness without harboring any desire to see him again.

My woman bits zing at thoughts of Tarrien. *Liar, liar.*

I shake my head and take a sip of my wine, wondering how quickly I can leave. People often think I must be an extrovert, standing up on stage every night, but it's actually the opposite. When I'm performing, I lose myself in the song. I love singing, for the pure joy of song itself and not just because it provides a release from my banshee magic. But I hate being the center of attention.

And right now, in the middle of a crowd that has gathered to honor my ten-year anniversary, all eyes on me, I feel far more anxious than usual.

Drink up, Dreya suggested, so that's what I do. I throw back the whole glass in a few large gulps, and someone laughs and presses another into my hand. I down that one, too, and then paste a large smile onto my face and move into the crowd, greeting the many who come up to wish me well.

I may not like being around crowds overly much, but these are still a decent bunch of people and as close to family as I've ever really known.

The memory of a set of hazel-green eyes staring almost directly into mine in the hallway of my building flashes in my brain, and I wonder what it would be like to actually meet one of my siblings. Or even, several of them? *Maewen*. She must be tough, to work with SUDAP when, presumably, she is as affected as I am by the call of death. She must face death practically every day in her job. How does she protect herself from what must be sheer hell? Why would she choose to put herself through such torture?

What was the other name Tarrien mentioned? *Aleah*. What is she like? He said she lives out in the country, on a farm somewhere. Has she done that deliberately, to reduce her interactions with people? Our mother has a lot to answer for, populating this world willy-nilly with half-banshees all over the place, and then leaving us to fend for ourselves in whatever way we can.

Would my half-sisters like *me*? Or would they think me prickly and brash and wish we weren't related at all?

I down a third drink and decide to get the welcome speech over with. I approach the corner stage that currently holds a quartet playing dance music. Before I can step up to join them at the waiting microphone, Brady, one of the male dancers from our troupe, drags me by the hand into the middle of the crowd on the dance floor.

'Time to let loose, Indie," he says, twirling me around with great aplomb.

Music from quartet washes over us and my muscles relax as the wine begins to take effect. It won't last. My fae blood means I'll process the alcohol a little more quickly than a human might, but for now, the tension that has held me tight for the past several months begins to dissipate at last.

I sink into the moment. The speech can wait. I even smile at Brady, and he takes the encouragement and steps close, sliding his arms tightly around my waist. I sway against him, wondering if he thinks it would be unhealthy to be with me. Judging by the growing hardness in his groin as he mashes it against me, I'm guessing he would be really keen to take it further.

I want to feel something for him in return, but I don't. Not one whit of desire. It feels like I'm dancing with my brother. What is wrong with me? I'm half drunk, in a cozy club, being held close by a handsome man, and all I can think about is my desperate need to see Tarrien again.

My thought patterns are so annoying I tip my head to the side and let Brady nuzzle at my neck. I so want to feel something—anything—but my body remains unstirred—until I stare over the top of the nuzzling guy's head, and meet a stormy silver-gray gaze directing fiery judgement my way.

Tarrien? What the devil is he doing here?

My heart jumps and my whole body switches on as if I've just stuck my finger in an electric socket. Moments ago, I was craving desire, trying to prove a point to myself. Just like that, knowing he's in the club and only meters away, there's an instant ache between my legs and the delicious flutter of butterflies in my belly.

God damn it! Why does that fae—and *only* that fae—have such an effect on me?

To my horror, a tiny moan escapes me and my dance partner squeezes tight, thinking my reaction is due to him.

"No, please." I struggle in Brady's arms, trying to push him away. "I need to—"

"My turn now, sir." Tarrien steps smoothly between us, wrestling me neatly out of the other man's grip and twirling me away until we reach the far side of the dance floor.

"What on earth—"

"You looked about as happy as if you were sitting in a dentist's chair, ready to face the drill," he says.

I raise a brow at the analogy. My banshee blood means I've been lucky enough to never need a dentist, but from what I've heard from my human friends over the years, he's probably not far wrong. I don't need to admit that to him out loud.

"So, you decided to swoop in and rescue me?"

"I am a warrior, after all. Rescue is my thing."

He says it with such seriousness that a chuckle pops out before I can stop it.

"Your thing?"

"Yes. And that's better. Now your smile is genuine."

Despite my annoyance with him, and confusion as to what he's doing here, I can't help but realize he's right. For the first time since I arrived, I actually feel genuinely at ease, and it has nothing to do with alcohol.

"All right. You win. I admit that I'm not...*displeased* to see you, warrior. But why are you here, Tarrien? Where did you go, and why have you reappeared now?" A thought strikes me, and my grin becomes a frown. "Has something else happened in relation to... you know?"

I don't feel like I can mention the abominations in the middle of this crowd, but he knows what I'm asking.

"No. At least, nothing that I'm aware of. And I never went anywhere. I've been keeping a discreet distance all week, but I've been making sure you're safe. I—"

"Wait." I stop swaying to the music and pull back from him. "You've been following me? Since that night? Sneaking around and spying on me?"

His eyes flare with what looks like irritation. "I'm not a sneak. Nor am I a spy. I'm simply doing my job—as a *protector*—and ensuring that you remain safe."

I want to be angry with him. I *should* be angry with him. It's creepy to know I've been going about my normal life—and missing him intensely—while he has been there all along in the shadows watching without my knowledge. But he seems to honestly care whether or not I'm safe, and as much as I want to tell him off, I manage to bite my tongue.

I'm not used to someone else caring about my safety and wellbeing. Even if his care comes from a place of duty rather than any other reason, at least it's there. And it's real.

Just as I open my mouth to make a joke about how his icicles must be back in place if he's able to protect me so dutifully, he lifts a hand and caresses my cheek. The words freeze in my throat, but everything else turns hot. That touch does not feel like duty. My shiver is one borne of desire, not cold, and I suck in a shaky breath and hold it far too long.

One corner of his mouth curves up in a sardonic grin, as if recognizing and approving my reaction. "I reappeared, as you put it, because it seemed like the right time. You seem less angry than you've been all week, and I've been wanting to say something to you ever since the last time we spoke."

Wow. He really has been keeping a close eye on me all week, then.

His gaze softens. "Indie, I really wanted to apologize for—"

His voice is cut off by the sound of a huge

explosion. Then a whole series of smaller explosions follow and the noise and smoke and flashes of light turn everything in the club into utter chaos.

Tarrien

STUN GRENADES. Human ones, at that, but no less of a threat, because where there are flashbangs, trouble is sure to follow. Plus, the majority of the crowd here are human and therefore far more fragile in terms of their mortality than Indie or me.

I can't worry about the others. I push Indie to the ground and throw myself over the top of her, intending to create a protective bubble. Before I can cast the magic, a deep growl reverberates through the screams and chaos and the tripping and falling humans all around us. Then another growl, lower and even more menacing than the first, and I realize there are two loups in the building, and they are stalking us.

Stalking *her*, to be accurate.

Even through the chaos of running people, smoke from the grenades and the dim lighting in the room, two sets of eyes, red tinged with purple, are visible. Both sets are clearly fixed on Indie. Werewolf shifters, with the twisted promise of madness evident in their features. No modicum of civility or reason is left in these two, even though they have retained the half-form often preferred by their kind at the time of the full moon. Part man, part beast. No humanity.

My heart rate speeds up. Not because I can't take these two—I can, of course—but because I'm not sure I can do so effectively while keeping an eye on Indie. I doubt these two loups used human flashbangs, which means they are not the only attackers.

The stakes seem so much higher now than when Lady Renna first gave me this assignment.

"Stay down," I whisper in her ear, "and get yourself under one of those tables. I'll take care of these abominations and come back for you."

"What table? I can't see a goddamn thing after those flashes." She rubs her face and then stares around. "Except for those awful reddish-purple eyes. I can see those. Unfortunately."

Her half-human senses must have been affected by the flash. Luckily, being full-fae, I am immune.

"Blink hard a few times. Your sight will come back in a minute or so. There are two loups about to launch, over there to your right where you can see those eyes. I need you to drop completely to the floor and roll away, to your left."

"No, wait, I—" She grabs at my arm but I have to trust that she'll do as I say. I can't fight them from down here on the floor.

"Now!" I yell.

Indie drops and rolls. I jump to my feet and swivel to face the twin abomination threat. One of the giant creatures launches at the spot just vacated by Indie. I drop the surface glamor I had donned for the party, and call for my armor and weapons.

Metal fills my fists and I twirl as fetid breath and a spray of hot mucus fans across my face. Indie is gone, thank the winter gods. I can only hope she's sheltering under one of the club tables.

The loup swivels back and roars in rage. We are only about eighteen inches apart. I can't use my sword in here, not with all these humans rushing back and forth in panic. Close work calls for the dagger.

I thrust forward and up with my silver blade, burying it to the hilt in the chest of the were.

For a moment, we are eye to eye, and I stare deep into that bloodshot gaze, looking for a trace of its soul. Nothing remains but darkness, and pain, and rage, beneath a strange purple miasma that roils inside the creature like an oily ooze.

Why won't it fall?

"Damn you!"

The abomination's top lip curls up on both sides, to reveal canines almost four inches in length. *Not good.*

"You will not stop us, fae," the were hisses. "We will get her in the end. We will get *all* of them."

"Not while I live!"

I twist the knife as the creature opens its mouth wide—wider than my head—and readies itself for the kill. I drop the sword and grab another silver dagger from my etheric arsenal. This one I angle up and into its throat. The start of a roar becomes instead a wet gurgle. Blood gushes up and out of its mouth, coating me and the floor, as a piercing wail on the edges of my consciousness begins to make itself heard.

Indie? Has my action just set off her banshee cry?

The wail rises, hurting my ears, as the were collapses to the floor, dead. Quickly, I pull out the daggers and turn, looking for the other monster. It hovers over the table that Indie has managed to roll beneath. The giant head bends and sniffs at her with that half-wolf, half-human snout. She is curled up into a tiny ball, rocking back and forth, wails still slipping out of her. She is obviously in the throes of a death call.

Is that still for the were? Or are there others around us who have been injured or killed in the melee?

I cannot afford to remove my gaze from the abomination to see what else is happening around us. I stagger toward them, slipping in the dead loup's blood and stumbling sideways. The other one's gaze snaps to me.

Good. Keep looking at me, abomination. Don't you dare go near the banshee.

The monster launches toward me in a huge leap. I don't quite have enough purchase on the blood-soaked floor to twist away in time. It lands squarely on my chest, the weight of it knocking me backward into the edge of the bar. Hot breath and one of its canines grazes my neck as I arch away and stab blindly.

Bullseye. Somehow, I manage to slide my dagger

between two ribs directly into its heart. The monster is already dead when it collapses on top of me. By the time I manage to push it off and leave the carcass propped over the bar, I realize I can no longer hear Indie crying. Shouldn't she be singing about the second abomination's death? Shouldn't I be able to hear her above everyone else in this crazy, smoke-filled room?

I turn toward the table that sheltered her, and she's no longer there.

As I swivel back and forth, searching frantically for a sign of where she might have disappeared to, the overhead lights switch on fully and a team of SUDAP-suited police officers rush in. Leading the way is a woman who looks almost exactly like Indie. Similar, and yet different. Maewen. The sister.

She stops short when she sees me. I'm no doubt a horrific sight, covered in loup blood and still sporting my winter warrior armor. Her eyes narrow and she points a finger directly at me.

"Grab that one first," she directs two members of her team. "And use the special cuffs."

Indigo

THE DEATH CALL is still upon me when multiple sets of hands drag me out from beneath the table and across the floor of the club. These aren't abomination hands, or paws, or claws. They are human hands, and they are dragging me along the floor against my will.

There are too many of them to fight off. I kick and wriggle as much as I'm able, given the keening call of death has turned me to jelly. One of them picks me up and throws me over his shoulder. Before I can say anything between the crying bouts, I find myself out the door and on the street, being bundled into the trunk of a large black car.

Just before the lid of the trunk is slammed shut, I catch a glimpse of a team of police officers rushing into the club. Is that…Maewen? My sister? Why is she not pretzeled up like me, crying at the deaths that befell some of those in the club?

At least she'll be there to help Tarrien. *Oh God. Tarrien! He's facing those abominations on his own. Will he survive?*

A blast of powerful heat washes over me. Is that magic? It doesn't feel like anything I've ever experienced before. Another blast and my vision fills with purple, even in the confines of the trunk.

What is happening? What…?

My thoughts disintegrate into nothing.

Chapter Six

I blink and rub my eyes. Where am I? What happened? Memories tumble back in and I start to sit up, only to bump my head. I am still in this goddamn car trunk. Fear and anger war in my chest, both causing my heart rate to speed up.

At least the banshee cry has calmed. It must mean we are now quite a way from the club—or anywhere else where people might be dying.

Tarrien, I hope you're okay. I hope you ripped those abominations to shreds.

Worrying about Tarrien and all my human friends —my almost-family, as I'd been thinking of them only minutes before the attack—will not help my current situation. I try to put the worry to the back of my mind, and wriggle around the space looking for something I might be able to use as a weapon.

Nothing, of course. Not even a tire iron. Whoever

these people are, they came prepared. Not to kill me, as now seems obvious. At least, not immediately. They must want something from me first, and it appears that they'll do anything to get it. Even hurt or kill my human workmates.

I contort myself so I can reach my stiletto heels in the tiny space, grateful they somehow stayed on my feet during the initial attack. I feel more in control with something in my hand, even if it is just a spiky shoe heel.

These suckers can take out an eye, I figure, so in the end I remove both shoes, clutching one in each hand, and wait. As I do, I make a mental note to myself. If I get out of this alive, I am ordering a special delivery of shoes that feature spiked silver heels, preferably wrapped around a core of wood. That should cover many of my bases when it comes to those abomination creatures.

I hear voices muttering from inside the car and I roll closer toward the back seat, trying to piece together what they're saying. Even though it is muffled, here in the trunk, I can make out a few words here or there. But none of them make any sense. It sounds like they are talking in a language I've never heard before. Given languages are a hobby of mine, and I can speak seven of them fluently, I don't understand.

Is it *fae*? Is it the language of my mother's people? In all the years of dabbling in language classes, I've deliberately steered clear of that one. Now, I wish I hadn't been quite so quick to spite my fae heritage. If I'd swallowed my pride, I might know something of what my kidnappers plan next. Instead, I remain in the dark, literally and figuratively.

I remember the last attack and what the abomination said. It wanted my name. My real name. If I give them my real name—the one Mother told me about all those years ago and that I can hardly remember, now—will they leave me alone? Will they leave my friends and work colleagues alone? Will they leave Tarrien alone—presuming he's still alive, that is.

My gut says they won't. My gut is telling me that these people are playing for the highest of stakes, and once they have what they want, they will discard me, and everyone I care about, like trash.

I will not let that happen again. Not this time.

I'm not sure how, but I'm going to get myself out of this predicament, and I'm going to fight with everything I have.

As I come to that conclusion, the rocking motion of the car begins to slow and I guess we must have reached our destination. Wherever that is.

The engine switches off and silence fills the air, but it is not the pleasant silence of peace. Instead, tension cuts across the nothingness, and my fear escalates as footsteps click on a hard surface outside before the snick of the lock on the trunk sounds.

As the lid begins to open, I launch myself up with a feral scream. Banshees can scream louder than most, and I do have the advantage of surprise in this instance. I channel all my angst and terror into that scream. The man who opened the trunk staggers backward, clutching at his chest, before a determined look removes the shock that briefly colored his features.

Quickly, I scrabble out of the trunk, swiping left and right with my shoe weapons. The banshee scream continues as a second man rushes around from the other side of the car. The two of them advance in formation, both wincing as the banshee cry continues to assault their ears.

They look so ordinary and human. Surely, these were not the ones who disabled a whole room full of people including a fae winter warrior, no less, and then blasted me with some kind of powerful purple magic?

As I stare at them with a confused frown, another blast of that oily-feeling magic washes over me. I drop the stilettos and fall to my knees, retching. *What is this*? It feels as if someone is sucking out my insides through my belly button, one small piece at a time. I gasp for breath, the pain so crippling I can no longer make even the slightest squeak, let alone a full-throated banshee cry.

A third male rounds the corner of the car, and I can tell instantly this one is no ordinary human. He glows with magic. Purple magic. It would be a beautiful sight, were it not so utterly terrifying.

Guess I'll have to cross purple off my list of favorite colors.

I've heard the rumors, like most beings in this post-Accord world. Though the supernaturals came out of hiding thirty or so years ago and struck an agreement to live amicably together with humans, there are some who would still prefer to keep the species separated. Scratch below the surface of the Accord and there will always be a few who talk about the loss of power that "coming out" forced upon them. Those rumors have been gathering momentum recently, even making the TV news on occasion. For some reason, the necromancers have been at the center of those rumors.

I always imagined a necromancer as an old, withered, gray-haired man, wearing a gown and a pointy hat. This guy is dark-haired, wearing normal human street clothes, and would be handsome were it not for the scarily blank expression on his face as he stares down at me in concentration.

Steer clear of the purple magic, everyone says. *Necromancer magic. Never trust a necromancer.*

Which makes my current situation, kneeling in front of a person who oozes that cloying purple magic, all the more chilling. He positions himself so that, to anyone watching, it would appear that I'm about to give him a blow job. Though it is unlikely that anyone will see us. From our surroundings, I would judge we're still in the city, and the car has been parked in a dead-end alley way.

No one is likely to pass by and come to the rescue, and I can't move away from him on my own. He has frozen me in place. Bastard. He knows exactly how to make a woman feel helpless.

His smile is wide but contains no mirth whatsoever. The eyes are cold and calculating, and he clearly enjoys my fear and discomfort.

"Well, well, banshee songstress. We meet at last. You and your little country bumpkin sister have been rather difficult to...shall we say, connect with."

Country bumpkin? Is he talking about Aleah? You go, girl, I silently applaud her efforts to evade this bastard. She obviously did a better job of that than me. If I ever survive this, I'm going to make an effort to meet her. Maybe Maewen, too.

My stomach flip-flops at the realization I may never get the chance to meet my sisters. Or even find out how many other of my mother's children are out there in the wider world.

I refuse to give in to the fear, even if his goddamn magic suffocates me in the process. I still cannot rise, but his magical iron grip on my throat has eased and I narrow my eyes and glare up at him.

"Who are you and what the hell do you want with me?"

"Ah, the million-dollar question. Or rather more likely, the trillion-dollar question, by the time we end this and get what we need."

My heart is pounding so hard I'm sure he can see it

vibrating in my chest. "I'm not giving you anything, wizard. You can try, but I won't cooperate."

His grin widens. "We don't need you to give us anything, young lady. We'll just take what we need. Your cooperation will make things less protracted and painful for you, but even without it, our plans are well in train. And now that we have you, we can progress things more quickly."

I struggle in earnest then, but it does no good. His magic has my knees pinned to the ground.

Tarrien, I call out in my mind. *Where are you? I'll let you follow me to the ends of the earth and back again—forever—if you just materialize now and smite this guy's head right off his shoulders. I'll even kick it like a football once you're done.*

My knight in shining armor doesn't appear.

Instead, the necromancer raises his hand and the miasma hits me right in the face. The force pushes all the air right down to the base of my lungs, stopping my breathing, and sends my thoughts and my senses into chaos. In the jumble, I feel myself lift from the ground, swirling as if caught in a freak whirlwind, and then a moment of dark nothingness descends. The transition is too brief to evoke terror.

When the darkness ends and I begin to see flashes of light, I blink several times, gasping for breath. Then I stumble and put out a hand.

Cold. Icy cold. I stare around me at a winter wonderland lit by moonlight: ice and snow and trees bare of leaves but arching up toward the stars in a strange kind of beauty nonetheless. My kidnappers didn't accompany me through the blackness. I am standing here on my own.

The hand I had thrust out to halt my fall is resting on a stone wall topped with a dusting of snow. The surface beneath my fingers thrums with energy. The wall itself circles around a large clearing in front of a turreted building. It appears to be a smallish castle made of stone, with a grand entrance that should look inviting, but it doesn't.

There is something seriously off about that castle and this forest scene, but I can't quite put my finger on it. It has nothing to do with having been kidnapped and forced through some kind of travel portal against my will. No, it is the actual place itself that sends shivers down my spine and ignites dread deep down inside.

Death reigned here, and not too long ago. The essence of it calls to the banshee within me, but the pull is not strong enough to bring forth the banshee song. Whoever died here, is gone, though the disturbing trace remains.

Where in the hell am I?

Is this a fae glamor laid over the top of the urban environment I just came from? If I squint my eyes, will I see something different beneath? I try it out. Nothing changes, but the feeling of wrongness intensifies, and I fancy I can see a tinge of purple hanging over the landscape. So, not a fae glamor, but perhaps instead a necromancer gathering place protected by a purple-tinged spell?

Or is this place something else altogether? Wherever they've dumped me, this is definitely not Melbourne anymore. Considering the energy thrumming beneath my palm in the very stones of the place, I don't think this is even the human realm at all. I remove my hand from the wall and take a few steps forward, toward the castle. Given how my human half is shrinking in anxiety and my banshee senses have just sharpened significantly, I think I might be in Faerie.

Tarrien

INDIE'S SISTER paces back and forth in front of me, barking orders into a mobile telephone, her scowl marring the beauty of her features.

When she finally ends her call and shoves the phone into the holder on her jeans, she turns to face me. "Are you going to tell me what happened here? Why a fae decked in warrior armor is hanging out in a cabaret club in Melbourne? And how you came to be covered in so much blood?"

I expect her to sound like Indie, but her voice is rougher, less refined. Perhaps that is due to Indie's voice training for her job as a singer; perhaps it is simply that this banshee works with the police and her days are spent rubbing shoulders with those less salubrious than Indie's theater folk.

I hold out my hands, silently requesting release from the cuffs. I can't access my magic while these things manacle my wrists, but at least they cuffed me at the front and not behind my back.

Use the special cuffs, she had ordered, and use them they did. Whatever power is contained in these cuffs, it muffles my fae magic until I can barely feel it at all.

I have the inbuilt physical strength to bust the manacles apart, but that would likely injure those humans still milling around us, and it will be much less catastrophic if she simply lets me free herself.

"Oh no," she says, with a grin that doesn't reach her eyes. "You speak first, and then I'll decide whether to release you from those."

"Very well." What is it with Lady Renna's daughters? Why are they all so frustrating to be around? I unclench my jaw and work it to release the tension.

"I am a warrior of the Winter Court, and I have been tasked—by your mother, in fact, Maewen—to protect the guest of honor at the event held here this evening."

"The famous club singer, Indigo?" She has obviously already spoken to several of the guests—the ones not injured or killed in the initial blast and attack

—to ascertain that the party was held in honor of Indie.

"Indeed," I answer.

"And you say my mother gave you the task to protect her?" She shakes her head and continues before I can answer. "Putting aside the fact that I don't wish to acknowledge that woman as my mother, why would the fae who birthed me want to protect Indigo?"

I study her angry eyes and decide not to argue with her about Renna. Indie is the important focus right now.

"Your sister Indigo has been the target of a number of attacks recently, by abominations. Rogue supes that are almost certainly created and controlled with necromancer magic."

"I know what abominations are. We've been dealing with them all over the place recently. But..." She tilts her head and studies me. "*Sister*? What do you mean, my sister? Indigo? She's my...*sister*?" Her voice ends on a squeak.

"Of course. Have you not studied yourself in a mirror lately? You are very similar in looks. I would have thought it obvious. But that's beside the point. We're wasting time. If you free me, I can head after her. They grabbed her in the melee. I can't sense her with these on, but if you set me free, I can use my fae magic to find her. I will *not* harm her. I give you my word as a winter warrior."

She huffs out a breath and I hold out my hands again to forestall the words I know she's about to utter.

"This is *werewolf* blood, not human. I killed those two loups your team is currently photographing, before they got to Indie. Unfortunately, while I was engaged in battle with the second, I believe Indie was snatched."

"You believe? Did you witness her being taken?"

I purse my lips in self-annoyance. "I did not. However, I think those who took her were likely human. They may have had someone with magical skills assisting them from afar—a wizard or necromancer, perhaps? But definitely not more than two abominations here in the club. I would have sensed them, otherwise."

Maewen runs a hand through her hair, messing it up despite the fact that the bulk of it is pulled back into a plait. She seems tired.

"Part of me wants to drag you off to the station and interrogate you some more," she says. I open my mouth to object when she adds, "But your story checks out. It's the same one that several of our witnesses have described. Two humans died—but one looks to have had a heart attack and the other was unfortunately trampled in the melee when everyone tried to get out. So, the only bodies that would produce as much blood as you are sporting right now, are the two dead loups."

She is silent so long after that, I feel compelled to speak. "You're welcome."

"You are a very annoying person."

"Your sister would agree with you, I think."

She glares at me with eyes that are so similar to Indie's a pang forms in my chest. *I hope my little banshee is okay.* Wherever she is, I hope she can hang on till I get there. I hope she won't need my healing powers the way Aleah did not so long ago.

"Did you happen to see any medallions on those loups you killed?" she asks.

"Medallions?" I frown, playing back the battle in my mind. "You mean, like a coin…"

"A necklace, with a big fancy-ass disk on the end of the chain."

"I do not think so."

"Hmm. Okay." She taps her teeth with a fingertip, thinking. "If the singer *has* been taken by—"

"Your *sister*, you mean?"

She makes a strange harrumphing sound. "That remains to be seen. I can't afford personal distractions right now. If the *singer* has been taken by those involved with the abomination attacks, then I guess we need all the help we can get in locating her."

"You are more like your mother than Indie."

She steps forward and produces a key, making quick work of the cuffs. "I met Renna once, and you and I both know you did not mean that as a compliment, Fae."

"I did not."

Luckily, my petty snipe does not deter her. As soon

as those cuffs are off my wrists, my fae magic rushes back in as if it were waiting in the corners of the room for my release.

I feel normal once again, and I release my hold on the warrior armor, allowing the glamor of human-styled street clothes to appear. I could have achieved cleanliness like this when I was with Indie in her apartment instead of using her shower, but for some reason, I wanted her to see the real me instead of anything simply conjured by glamor.

"Thank you, Maewen," I say. "I will find her, and I will do everything in my power to keep her safe."

I realized this week, while watching Indie go about her usual business, that my feelings for her are growing. I don't understand why. We had only the one night together. We still barely know each other. And yet, the thought of anything happening to her—at any time but especially on my watch—is completely unbearable.

"You'd better," Maewen says, and swivels away to answer a query from another SUDAP member. Just before I leave by touching the ring on my thumb, she turns back. "And it's not Maewen. It's Inspector Jones to you."

I leave Inspector Jones to the messy scene in the club and transport myself outside to the street, but of course, there is no actual physical clue left by now to indicate which direction Indie's kidnappers took her. I didn't think the attackers would be that stupid, but I had to check.

I reach out into the ether, searching for Indie's essence. Frustration fills me when I can't sense her at all. A sudden thought hits and my frustration morphs into anxiety. What if she's already...*no. Don't think like that.* She's strong and feisty, and whoever they are, they clearly don't want their banshee captive dead straight away. She will still be alive. She has to be. There is no other acceptable outcome than to have Indie safely back where she belongs.

And where is that? A tiny voice whispers in my head. Does she belong back here, in her ordinary human-based life? Or does she belong with you, in Faerie...in your arms?

Wherever she is, I need Indie to answer my call.

Silence is the only response. Nothing. It is as if she has been snuffed out like she never existed at all.

Chapter Seven

INDIGO

If this is Faerie, I didn't expect it to feel so...*forsaken.* It's the only word that fits this dark and lonely landscape. I'm aware of Faerie, of course, having listened to Mother babble on without stopping during her one and only visit when I was young. I've never been to see the place, but even knowing my roots are in the Winter Court, my mental image was one of vibrancy and icy beauty rather than the heavy trepidation that infuses me now.

Tarrien, is this where you're from? Is this why your heart is encased in ice and you say you cannot love?

At the thought of my warrior, my pulse rate briefly speeds up. If we are in Faerie, surely, he'll find me soon. *Please find me. I could do with some of your protection, right about now.*

The feel of that oily miasma hangs heavy in the air, making my breathing more labored than usual.

A man dressed in black ceremonial-style robes emerges from the shadows at the edge of the clearing. He strides toward me through the snow-covered landscape. It isn't one of those who snatched me from the club, but his face is grim and I suspect from his demeanor he's going to be as soulless as the others.

That's when I realize there are several figures lurking around the edges of the clearing. I study them, trying to work out who they might be. Are they all necromancers? Oh. *Dear heavens.* Some of these creatures look like abominations.

Great. I'm likely somewhere in the depths of Faerie, away from everyone and everything I've ever known, and it seems as though I've been brought to a necromancer stronghold filled with the very creatures I've been trying to escape.

"Hiya," I say, as the man draws to a halt in front of me.

He backhands me across the face. "The only thing I want to hear from you, banshee, is your name."

Ouch! I touch my stinging cheek and do a quick mouth explore with my tongue, hoping none of my teeth have been knocked loose. Nope. Teeth are all intact.

"Nice to meet you, too." *Oh, my God. Stop being a smart arse.* My head has the right attitude, but stress keeps making my mouth run off with itself. "Want my name? It's Indigo."

Another backhand.

"Your *real* name."

I narrow my eyes at him and this time I manage to press my lips together, successfully holding back more stupid words. Is my cheek already beginning to bruise or swell? Feels like it. That second whack really hurt.

He stares at me, during which time the others draw closer until a ring of black-robed figures circles us. Some are human and some are not, but at least the abominations aren't jumping in and ripping me to pieces. Yet.

Even as that thought touches my mind, one of the loups—a weirdly formed half-vampire, half-human hybrid—lurches forward and grabs me around the throat. I scrabble at its clawed hands, trying to loosen the hold, and shove my knee up into its groin area.

It just laughs, and squeezes tighter until no air can get through at all and pressure builds in my head. Then it leans in close to my face. The eyes gleam red with a hint of purple and its tongue darts out to caress its own incisors—up and down until I want to vomit at the sick innuendo.

Lucky my throat is closed off. The vomit can't get out.

Blackness films my vision as I begin to lose consciousness. Regret fills me at the thought of never properly meeting my sisters. Or getting to know Tarrien better. *Who else is going to chip away at the ice around your heart, Tarrien, and teach you how to love?*

I'm clearly losing my mind at the lack of oxygen.

Just as I decide this is the end of everything, and

wonder if I will experience the banshee call of my own death, a sharp voice calls out to stop. The pressure releases and I collapse onto the snow-covered ground, clutching at my neck and drawing long, labored breaths into my starved lungs.

It takes several minutes before I begin to recover, during which time they all talk among themselves in a language with which I'm not familiar. I imagine blasting them all with my banshee song and shattering their ugly black hearts into a million pieces. Only thing is, my banshee voice is unlikely to work as well as it should, now that my throat has been squeezed so much.

The man I assume to be in charge—the necromancer who first approached—finally hauls me to my feet.

"It's time." Disgust colors his tone. "Take her inside and prepare her for—"

"Not just yet." Another voice cuts over the top of the wizard, rendering him silent.

It is a female voice, one that sends shivers of delight across my skin. Judging by the reaction of everyone else in the clearing—even the loups—they all feel the same sense of pleasure that I just experienced.

A stunningly beautiful fae woman with white-blonde hair, wearing a long silver dress, strolls into the center of the circle and everyone drops to their knees and bows their heads. Even the man who I thought was in charge does the same, though admittedly he is the last to bend the knee.

Who is she, this tall woman with the incredible voice who can command even loups to grovel in the snow at her feet?

She smiles down at me and again, pleasure washes through my system. "Are you not going to bow before your queen, Indigo?"

My queen? Even as my mind scrabbles to try and figure out what's going on, I find myself dropping to my knees and bending my head, embarrassment swirling through me that I hadn't thought to do that the moment I saw her. She deserves reverence, this beautiful queen of mine.

Wait, what? I don't have a queen. Well, I do, but she's human and lives in England. This is not my queen. Why am I grovelling before her, filled with shame that I didn't drop the second I saw her?

I raise my head and stare up into her face, calling on everything within me to resist the urge to face-plant at her feet. Her facial features are perfectly formed, the expression warm and dancing with joy and her rosy lips tipped up in a welcoming smile. But there is something there in the depths of her icy blue eyes. I can't put my finger on it, but whatever it is feels dark and watchful. *Dangerous.*

Is this... no. It couldn't possibly be the Winter Queen. She was banished, many years ago from what

I've heard, and if that were the case, she would not be allowed back into Faerie at all.

If she has returned, the consequences for her and those who help her, would be quite severe. I remember reading something about it, once. I think the article mentioned death by execution if the queen and her accomplices ever returned.

But what do I know? My mind skitters again. I'm a half-banshee who has lived all her life in the human realm. I don't know anything about the fae and their ways. Not really. The articles I've read, and the TV shows I've watched, are just some human's version that has no real basis in truth. Maybe this isn't her at all, or if it is, maybe she was "unbanished" at some point, and I just didn't hear about it.

Maybe I got it all wrong, and she's not evil at all, but stepping in to try and rescue me from this group of necromancers and their abominable creations who clearly love to smack women around. I should be grateful to her for her wonderful presence...

I blink. What the hell? Is she manipulating my thoughts and emotions?

I stare deep into those beautiful eyes, and this time I see the lurking darkness for sure. Whatever it is slithers away the moment I connect with it.

I swallow back the flippant comment I was about to make, and instead, say carefully, "I am honored to be in your presence, Your Majesty."

It is the correct response. That dark watchfulness

recedes and her face lights up even more than it already is.

"Oh, you are much nicer than I was led to believe. Come, child. Rise, and walk with me a moment." She gestures at the necromancer when he makes a sudden movement to stop me getting to my feet. "Enough, Norrix. You can follow behind. For now."

Norrix? Hmm. No wonder the guy has attitude.

She takes my hand and tucks it into the crook of her arm, and together, whether I want to or not, we head toward the castle entrance.

Tarrien

DESPAIR BUILDS IN ME. I cannot sense her. I have cast my magic wide, over and over again, until a headache plagues my skull and all the muscles in my body are stretched so tight I feel like I might snap in half at any moment.

How is it possible that she has disappeared into a place I cannot reach? I have never failed in this, before.

I cast again, searching. Nothing.

I lean back on the settee in the apartment I use when in the human realm. It moves with me, depending on where I am at the time, and at present it is situated in Melbourne's redeveloped Docklands area. I have a balcony, and I have been enjoying the river view and the boats, and the cosmopolitan buzz of the crowds. To me, this area encompasses all things good about being in the human realm.

I can't concentrate on any of that tonight. I can't concentrate on anything, but trying to locate Indie. I shrug my shoulders up and down a few times to ease the tension. When did I last eat? The thought of food makes my stomach turn.

If I can't find her, I can't save her. And if I can't save her...

Where are you, Indie? If she is in the human realm, or even in Faerie, I should be able to feel her essence.

What if she dies, because I fail her? *What if she's already dead*? That would explain why I cannot find even the tiniest spark of her existence.

My heart skips a beat at the thought and then speeds up until I have to take deep breaths to calm my system.

This is not how an ice warrior should behave. We should be emotionless and calm, and do our duty without falling in a heap when things go awry. Is that why I can't sense Indie? Because I risked letting down my icy guard in making love with her, and now my magic is tainted and doesn't work as well?

I release a low growl. I cannot think that way. *Focus.*

I do not want to consider failure as an option. I cannot explain why the thought of Indie passing from existence terrifies me so much. Of course, it would mean that I had failed at my task of protection, but the fear that travels right to the marrow of my bones is about far more than simply failing at a job. If I have lost her, when we have only just met and begun to connect...

I'll just have to melt that ice around your heart, won't I? The memory of her playfully delivered words washes over me, as does the remembered feeling of joy her presence evoked. I stand and begin to pace the room. She cannot be dead. That is not a possibility I am willing to consider.

I must find her. I will. Somehow.

I cast one last time, already knowing the action will be futile but I can't seem to help myself. Tendrils of my power leach out, searching every corner of this world and my own. There are other realms, of course, but I cannot see why she would be taken anywhere other than here, or Faerie. Even the latter seems unlikely, given the clues regarding necromancer involvement and knowing their base is essentially here in the human realm.

After several minutes of futile seeking, I give up and stagger back to the couch, clutching my aching head in my hands.

What to do? Will Lady Renna be able to assist? Her position as a favored member of the Winter Court gives her power, and power infuses our magics, reinforcing and enhancing whatever is innate within us. Renna's magic is likely equally as strong as mine, if not stronger. Banshee fae are rare, particularly full-bloods, and there are whispers that hint at banshee power that has never been fully tapped.

Perhaps we could combine our efforts and find Indie that way. Surely, Renna would have an advantage, given Indie is her own flesh and blood.

Blood over... over what? What connection do I possibly have with Indie? *Lust*? It cannot be love. My mind skitters from that word as fast as it pops into my head. It is lust I feel for Indie, not love, and a blood bond between mother and child, no matter how long it has been since they saw each other, is surely stronger than any lustful connection I might have with the one I seek.

I touch the ring on my thumb, calling for Renna. The last thing I want to do is see that damn woman again, but I am unable to think of any other alternative.

I have to find Indie.

Renna, I scream silently through the ring. *Your daughter is in trouble. Get here, now.*

Lady Renna appears in my apartment, scowling as she hurriedly fastens buttons on her bodice top and straightens her diaphanous skirt. I avert my gaze, focusing on a point just beyond her shoulder. The banshee is not wearing undergarments.

"This had better be good, warrior," she says through gritted teeth. "I was about to mount my latest human conquest, and he has a cock bigger than many of his kind. I am most displeased at being summoned in such a way."

I release a growl and clench my fists, trying to control the instant dislike this woman ignites in me.

"Indie has been kidnapped, and I need your assistance to find her." The words are difficult to get out. I do not want to admit my failing to Renna, and I do not want to have to call on her for help.

Her eyebrows rise and her features slacken. "Can't you use your seeking magic to locate her?"

I jump to my feet and pace back and forth in front of her.

"Do you think I haven't *tried*?" I yell, before taking a few deep breaths to calm myself. "I *have* tried. Over and over. I cannot sense any aspect of her in either the human realm, or Faerie. I believe it was a group of necromancers who grabbed her. Is there anywhere else they may have taken her, Renna? I need to find her, and quickly."

She flutters a hand at her throat and for the first time since I've known her, Renna appears genuinely concerned for someone other than herself. "Her blood is very valuable to—"

"Yes, yes," I cut her off. "To vamps, I know. Hybrid blood sends them into paroxysms of pleasure. I saw that, with Aleah and her lover. What has that got to do with—"

"No, you don't understand. Banshee-human blood is one of the rarest of combinations. There is great power in her blood—in the blood of all my hybrid children, in fact. Not just for vampires, but for others, too. If they can ascertain her true name, they can access that blood power and use it...drain it... Oh, this is bad. This is very bad, indeed."

She takes a seat on my couch and begins to rock back and forth. I can't tell if she's upset in general terms, because the banshee power is at risk, or if her concern is more specific to Indie and her current wellbeing, or lack thereof.

I squat in front of her and snap my fingers to bring her attention back to me.

"Listen, Renna. You are very powerful, I know. I thought, perhaps, together, we could link our magics and search for her. We might have a better chance of seeking her out before..." I trail off, biting back the rest. *Before they kill your daughter. Unless they already have.*

Her gaze meets mine. "Yes, it is worth trying. But our magic is strongest at home. Not here." She glances around the room then and wrinkles her nose, as if noticing the sparse furnishings for the first time. "We need to return to Faerie. I can use a tracing spell from there, which will reach further than the human and fae realms, especially if I can boost it with your winter warrior's power. Wherever she is, I am sure we will be able to locate her."

I search her face, looking for any subterfuge, but see none. I don't trust Renna or her motives at all, but in this, she seems genuine about wanting to help Indie.

"All right. Return to Faerie, we locate Indie, and then I'll get her back."

Renna's gaze narrows. "You'd better." She pokes me in the chest. "If you do not find and rescue my daughter, I will ensure King Tryppton executes your mother and sister."

I jerk back in shock. "You would not."

"Try me. Banshee blood *cannot* be allowed into the wrong hands. Now, let's go." She reaches out and clasps my hand for the transition between realms. I am tempted to pull away, until I remember the futility of my own search for Indie.

I grit my teeth and nod, full of rage as I enter the space between realms. How dare she threaten my family? *How dare she!* Even though I know the Winter King would be unlikely to execute two innocent people, Renna's stupid announcement adds an extra layer of stress to the situation. As if I needed any more incentive to rescue the woman I... *lust* after.

Lust? Who am I kidding? It's a damn sight more than that. My mind sheers away from whatever it is we might have begun to develop and I try to concentrate on the here and now. All I know is, I have to get Indie back. I can't bear the thought of those monsters harming a single hair on her beautiful, stubborn head.

Hold on, Indie. I'm coming for you. I only hope I can get there in time.

Chapter Eight

INDIGO

The queen leads me through the entrance and into a great hall. There are rugs on the stone floor, and conversation areas with chairs set up in front of fires burning in several grates around the edge of the room. Despite the grandeur of the mini-palace, the effect is somewhat cozy.

And yet still, my skin crawls as we enter. Something evil lurks here, and I don't know what it is.

"Very nice, Your Majesty," I murmur, staring around for any hint of what might be giving me the heebie jeebies. "Is this your home?"

"This? Oh, no." She removes my hand from her arm and turns to face me. "This is merely temporary. My rightful home was stolen from me, but I intend to take it back."

At those last words, it is as if a veil drops away from

her features and the lurking darkness takes the fore. I step back, unable to help the recoil. She smiles as if she sees and enjoys my discomfort.

"You *are* the exiled Winter Queen, then," I confirm, though there can be hardly any doubt. I can't think of another royal fae who might consider their rightful place "stolen", nor who would be hiding out in a place so filled with obviously malicious intent.

She must have done something pretty seriously bad to be exiled, and from the malicious feel of her, it probably came naturally, whatever it was. For the first time, I wish I'd made more of an effort to learn the ways of the fae, and to understand a little more about my mother's people.

Her eyes flash at my statement. "I am Queen Rhiannon of the Winter Court, and as a banshee and member of my Court, you must bow to me."

Despite using all of my willpower, I can't stop myself dropping to my knees. I want to shriek at the sense of powerlessness she evokes in me. This is as bad as being caught in the call of the banshee, only worse. At least, the banshee cry is a natural phenomenon when you're actually half-banshee. This control she has over my body—and my emotions—is infuriating.

When I'm finally grovelling at her feet, whether I want to or not, her gaze turns sweetly curious once again. "What is your name, child?"

Oh, my God. This again?

"Indigo, Your Majesty." No way am I giving her the long version. *Indigosturianawella*, I think was what Mother told me, all those years ago. I tried it out a few times after she left, staring into the mirror in my bathroom, but my mouth could hardly wrap itself around the syllables and I felt too stupid to persist. In the end I decided Indigo—or Indie as my mostly human friends call me—would suffice.

The robed brigade from outside have crowded into the large domed room with us and I cringe, expecting another backhand. Nothing happens, until the queen bends forward and thrusts her face right into mine.

The dark thing dancing behind her icy gaze sends a quiver of terror right through me. "It will not matter whether or not you give us your true name. We can do this without it, but it will certainly be easier on you if you share your power through name rather than blood."

Um... "Blood?" *That doesn't sound promising.*

Tarrien, my mind screams. *If you want to protect me, now would be an awesome time to show up.*

Instead, the queen grabs my chin in an unforgiving pincer-like grip as the robed men and creatures draw closer around us.

"You're a hybrid, one of Renna's brats. Your voice as a banshee carries both life and death within its song. Do you not know that, girl?"

I do. If my heart weren't pounding so fiercely in my chest I might take the time to query her. What the hell does my banshee voice have to do with my name, or my blood? In the end, I keep quiet. I sense my time might be up very soon, and I don't want to die. Not here, not now, and not like this.

The queen's top lip curves up in a derisive snarl. "On second thoughts, do not provide your name. It will give me great pleasure to use blood from that banshee bitch's bloodline, to enact my plan."

She releases my chin and straightens, glaring around at our audience until she finds the man who was in charge before she arrived.

"Take her, and prepare her for the ritual. I will return in two hours and I expect her—and all of you—to be ready." With that she turns away in a swirl of silver and disappears into the ether.

I'll have to get Tarrien to teach me that one. If I survive past the next two hours. Would have been quite handy to disappear right about now.

The absence of the queen means the hold she had over my body is gone, and I stagger to my feet and face the leader of the robed group.

"Want me? Then you'll have to come and get me." I open my mouth and scream at them as loudly as I can.

Everyone in the room staggers back, clapping their hands over their ears. I keep the scream going, using everything innate within me, on top of everything I've been taught as a singer, to control the note until I hear glass shattering in the background. *Good!* When the groans of pain around me become audible—even through the scream—I turn and begin to run.

I ACHIEVE AN EMBARRASSINGLY short distance before one of the loups knocks into me from behind. I topple to the ground. It sits on top of my back, crushing my lungs with its weight, and sniffs greedily at the back of my neck with its disgusting wet muzzle. I almost retch right here on the fancy rug when a hot wet tongue licks my skin.

"You can have her after the ritual. If there's anything left." The voice above me is that of the lead necromancer. He is addressing the abomination on my back, but clearly, his words are designed to fill me with dread.

Instead of dread, hatred for him and his cronies suffuses my whole body. I have never felt more helpless, and never felt more motivated to hurt another human being. Even kill them, if I can, despite the fact that I will no doubt have to endure the banshee call of death. I am willing to put up with that, to rid the world of beings as evil as this bunch of monsters.

I might be fired up to hatred, but my situation doesn't bode well for being able to act upon it. Instead, the weight disappears off my back and I am unceremoniously hauled to my feet by a clawed hand.

A woman I hadn't noticed among the crowd steps forward and gestures to the abomination to bring me to her.

She is dark-haired and robed, like the men, and when she tosses back her hair, I notice her ears are rounded. She's not fae, then. Perhaps she is human, or part-human, like me. A witch? Whoever she is, I sense no avenue of assistance will be forthcoming. She exudes the same oily feel as the others.

She leads the way through the castle hallways and the abomination drags me along in her wake. The clawed grip on my upper arm remains unrelenting and provides no opportunity for escape. We head down a narrow set of stairs and through a large wooden door at the base, and then along more winding hallways until we reach a large, columned room in which a sunken pool sits in the middle. Purple-tinged steam rises from the water, and I almost choke at the cloying humidity. Two women, obviously servants by their submissive demeanor, are waiting by the edge of the pool with towels in their arms.

"Leave us now," the woman instructs the loup. "The room is protected and she cannot leave unless I provide permission."

It still seems strange to refer to the creature as a loup, even in my own thoughts. Loups are by definition supernatural creatures who have gone mad, and generally, they display no control or reason whatsoever. I notice a strangely patterned medallion around its neck and wonder if that has anything to do with its apparent obedience to these necromancers.

The loup who attacked me in the apartment building was wearing one of these... If I were to rip it off...

If it is the necklace keeping the loup obedient to its master or mistress, then me removing it would probably just result in my instant death, and probably the deaths of everyone else in this room, given what a normal loup is like.

Before I can fully decide one way or the other what to do, the loup is gone, and the woman moves to the door and barks instructions over my head.

"Bathe and clean her from top to toe, and then dress her ready for the ritual," the woman says to the other two. Then she turns her gaze on me. "If you resist, I will have these servants killed, and bring in two vampire loups to finish the job of bathing you. Either way it will be done, but if you resist, their deaths are on you. Do you understand?"

I glance at the two serving women, who are staring at me in fear. They know their fate lies in my hands, and now, I know it, too.

"Yes," I say through clenched teeth. "I understand."

"Good. Now hurry along and bathe. We don't have much time before Her Majesty will return, and you need to be ready."

Ready for what? What the hell is this ritual they keep speaking of? I have no opportunity to ask her any questions, because she disappears out the door and then slams it behind her.

I lunge at the door and wrestle with the handle, but it is locked. I stare wildly around, looking for another door, or a window, but there is nothing.

"Come, my lady." One of the women steps forward. "It is enchanted. You won't escape this room. Not unless they want you to. Now, why don't you undress and climb into this nice warm bath?"

As if in response to her words, the scent of lavender, and other herbs, and that underlying oily smell that permeates the very air we are all breathing, rises up like a creeping mist and curls its tendrils around me.

Despite the warmth in the room, I shiver. The last thing I want to do is immerse myself in that purple-tinted water, but it seems like I don't have any choice in the matter.

What the devil has that evil ex-queen planned for me?

Tarrien

WE ARRIVE BACK at Renna's quarters in the royal palace and I disentangle my hand from hers. She has brought us directly to her spell room, which should save us precious time.

To her credit, Renna moves quickly through the room toward a row of cupboards, and I begin to see that she is, in fact, concerned for her daughter. I am still annoyed by her threat to have my family killed, but I must put that aside for now if we are to do this, together.

"Tell me what you need," I say, staring around at the shelves of strange containers and old books. Fae magic is innate within us, though there are some, like Renna, who have also taken on more human practises such as those of witches or wizards. Or even necromancers. I scan the room, searching for any trace of purple, but nothing jumps out.

She pushes me aside and rushes to a wooden cupboard, withdrawing a container covered in strange markings.

"I only need this, and your power to amplify it," she says, bringing the container to a bench in the center of the room. "Come."

She beckons and I hurry across. She opens the container and tips it up, and a smooth gray stone drops to the bench. It is innocuous looking, though almost as big as her palm. When she picks it up and holds it, the stone begins to glow with a pale blue light.

"It's a tracing spell. I bought it from a witch many years ago, but have never had the need to use it, before now. Place your palm over the top, Tarrien."

I do as I am told.

"Good. Now that it is cradled within our palms, I

need you to concentrate. Do what you would normally do when seeking out someone's whereabouts. I will channel my magics through the stone at the same time, and together, we should be able to find Indigo. If she is still..."

Renna swallows, and for the first time ever, pity stirs within my breast when I look at her. She *does* care. Not in the way a normal mother should. Not in the way my mother has always cared for my sister and me. But it seems that I was wrong. Renna really does want Indie to be okay.

"We'll find her in time, Renna. I promise." I send out my magic, feeling the boost from her power through the stone, like a rush right through my veins. Does she feel the same, from me?

Renna's lips move as she whispers an incantation, and then, out of nowhere, I sense Indie's essence. It whispers through the ether, faint and nebulous, but it is there. I suck in my breath at the same moment Renna gasps and drops the stone.

"She's alive. I felt her, but..." I frown, unable to pinpoint exactly where she is. "I don't understand. It didn't feel like Faerie, and yet... it did. How is that possible?"

Renna rubs her palm, over and over, until I lean forward and gently stop the movement. She raises her eyes to mine, worry etched deep in their green depths.

"I felt her, too. She's in... the Badlands," she whispers, and my heart jumps.

No.

"They took her to the Badlands?" The halfway place, right on the edge between Faerie and the Nothing. Ruled by monsters and outlaws, of the worst kind.

Nausea rushes through me. I can't imagine a world—any world—in which Indie is snuffed out to nothing. And yet, if she takes a step in the wrong direction, trying to escape by herself...

"If she tries to get away from her captors, she could cross over into the Nothing, and cease to exist." Renna voices my concern and then grips the edge of the bench, hunching forward.

Against my instinct, I round the table and put my arm awkwardly across her shoulders. "I won't let her. Do you hear me? I will not let that happen, Renna."

She nods but doesn't meet my gaze. "I am sorry for what I threatened earlier. About your mother and sister."

Shock sends my eyebrows soaring skyward. Renna apologizing? That's a first. It shows the extent of her worry. Have I gotten her completely wrong, all these years? I am beginning to doubt my own views on everything, thanks to these contrary banshee women.

I squeeze her a little. "I will get her back."

I have to. The alternative is unthinkable.

"Once you are in the Badlands, you will sense where she is. You will be able to find her, Tarrien. But you need to hurry. Please."

I release Renna and reach for my ring. I am going to require assistance for this search and rescue mission. I will need several of my fellow winter warriors on board—those with the greatest power to resist the call of evil. Especially if we're heading into the Badlands.

Time to go to war.

Chapter Nine

INDIGO

In the end, I acquiesce quietly, stripping off and bathing as quickly as I can, refusing to let either of the women touch me. I have to admit, the warmth of the purple-tinged water is more soothing than I expected. When I climb out of the pool—I can't call it a bath; it's too large—one of the women hands me a fluffy white towel.

I stare around, looking for my clothing that I left in a pile at the edge of the pool. Nothing.

"Where are my clothes?" I wrap myself in the towel and raise a querying brow at the woman.

"You won't need them, dear." The other woman materializes out of the shadows. She has a long satin gown draped across her arms. "Here, you can wear this instead."

"Yeah." I eye the plunging neckline and sheer

nature of the fabric as she holds it up. "I don't think so. Give me back my own clothing, please."

The woman's mouth turns down in disapproval. "They are gone. It's either wear this, or appear in front of the conclave naked, and that wouldn't be very nice, now, would it?"

Right. I purse my lips, trying to hold in a curse word.

"Well," I say at last. "Judging by the look of *that*, there's not much difference between the two options. But I guess I don't have a choice."

I'm getting a little sick of having my right to choose taken away from me.

I wonder what she means by conclave. Is this a necromancer stronghold, and the conclave is their group meeting? A shareholder's meeting, wizard-style.

Why is a fae queen—an ex-communicated one, at that—here and apparently calling the shots? Necromancers are a secretive breed, from what I understand. Full of pride and powerful in their own right. Why would they kowtow to a banished fae royal?

The whispers over the years about evil intentions and bad magic have always been just that. Whispers. Rumors. I've never had any call to pay attention. I've never even met a necromancer before. Unless...

Was it wizard magic that killed my friend six months ago? Courtesy of a piloted loup? The seeds of that idea were already planted in my mind after the attack on my neighbor. Now, those seeds have sprouted, and the reality that Sienna probably died *because* she was my friend, sends ripples of horror through my system.

At the time, I believed the police who decided it was a random attack. Though I blamed myself for a long time, my therapist helped me understand that what I was experiencing was likely survivor's guilt, which is not uncommon in situations like that.

Sienna and I had just left the theater after a show and planned to head across the street for drinks at the cabaret club. We were standing on the sidewalk, chatting, when I realized I'd forgotten my wallet. I ran back inside to retrieve it from my dressing room, and was on my way out again when the banshee call struck.

Calling in the death of my best friend was by far the worst moment of my life.

By the time I was able speak coherently and stagger back outside, it was too late. Sienna was dead, her throat a mangled mess and one of her ears torn off. A crowd of horrified onlookers had formed around her body, which is likely why the killer ran off. It was deemed by the police as an interrupted robbery, though why a thief would take the time to bite out her throat but leave her handbag lying on the street next to her, was a question that remained unanswered.

As I collapsed beside her that night, still sobbing and crooning in the wake of the banshee cry, it seemed to me that an unpleasant purple haze lay over my friend. It eventually dissipated in the night breeze, and I hadn't thought any more about the haze. Until now.

A necromancer killed my friend. Which means... it wasn't a random attack. They were likely after me.

Fresh guilt washes over me, only this time, the guilt is laced with fury.

Who are these vicious monsters, and what the hell do they want?

The serving women slip the dress over my head, and when the fabric slithers down my legs and pools at my feet, I turn and study my reflection in the tall dressing mirror positioned off to one side of the room. Unfortunately, the mirror confirms that the dress is as see-through as I suspected. So much so, that I'm tempted to just rip it off once again and face whatever is coming buck-naked.

At least that might be less sexually enticing than the hints of nipple and bare mound that appear and disappear every time I move in this ridiculous outfit.

Is this going to be some kind of sex thing? Where a whole bunch of creepy men in ceremonial robes get off at the sight of the mostly naked banshee woman in a sheer dress?

Then I remember that some of those robed figures were abominations, and a wave of nausea hits me.

My heart speeds up and I clutch my hands together so the women can't see them trembling.

Hold on to the fury. It's safer to focus on that, than to fall apart in terror.

"Come, dear. Take a seat and we will dress your hair."

Oh, Dreya. I would give anything to be back in my small dressing room at the theater, my assistant bossing me around as she runs a brush through my hair and helps with my makeup.

If only I was there with you now, my dear friend.

The women drag a chair over to the dressing mirror and shove me down into it, and then both of them take turns to comb out my long hair and braid the edges into delicate little plaits.

I stare at my own reflection while they do their thing. My eyes are wide and scared, and the green color is brighter than usual. I guess they reflect the turmoil of emotions inside. I can barely contain my rage now. I feel as if I'm about to explode with the force of it. My cheeks are faintly flushed, and I can see the pulse at the base of my neck beating super-fast, which means these two women can probably see it too. I wonder if they know how riled up I am, and why. I clutch my hands even more tightly together in my lap, until my nails dig in to the flesh of my palms, forming little crescent marks.

Eventually the women finish doing my hair, and one of them comes around to face me and then darts out a hand to pinch my bottom lip hard between finger and thumb.

"Ow, Jesus!" I duck my head away and she makes a tsking noise.

"Just brightening up your mouth, dear. Now it's nice and plump and rosy."

Great.

"Don't touch me again," I say, and the two women laugh.

"We don't need to. You're as ready as you can be for the ritual, dear."

Double great. I grit my teeth and wait for the return of the queen. *Bring it on, bitches. I still have a voice, and this banshee is not afraid to use it.*

In the end, it isn't the queen who returns for me, but one of the hooded and robed men. At least it's not one of the loups. He doesn't speak, just looks me up and down and grins lasciviously. Then he gestures, and I march out ahead of him in the direction he indicates with my head held high and the heat of embarrassment in my cheeks.

I'm about to enter a whole room full of these monsters, and they'll likely all be staring at my privates, just like this guy. Ignore the leering, I tell myself. Think of it as a stage performance with an uncooperative crowd.

Easier said than done.

After heading down a long and winding set of stairs and along a corridor that has no windows, we reach a set of double doors. I presume we must be underground, and I hope the doors are not going to open up to reveal a rat-infested prison cell, or a dungeon.

No such luck. A prison cell would have been preferable to what greets me when the doors swing open and I march into the room ahead of my captor.

I stop short as a wave of illness washes over me. Death has touched this room, many times over. So much so, that even though the previous inhabitants passed over a while ago, the effects are strong enough to linger. I clutch at my belly, trying not to heave.

The space is cavernous, to the point that I can't even see a ceiling. The floor is made of stone, and tall pillars are dotted throughout the room, each pillar sporting a flickering candle lamp. Straight ahead of me is what looks like an altar, also made of stone. It could be a place of worship—though this is unlike any place of worship I've ever seen. The altar consists primarily of one huge, human-bed-sized slab, with purple candles decorating each corner.

In front of the slab, a fire pit ringed by a shallow stone wall has been arranged on the floor. Within the confines of the pit, a fire is already stoked and roaring. Above the fire an enormous black brazier bubbles and steams with a purple mist. Gathered around the fire and staring into the rising steam from the pot, are at least a couple of dozen robed figures, chanting in a language I don't recognize.

If I was scared before, it is nothing to the dread that fills me now. The chant sends chills across my skin and I freeze. What are they going to do with that pot? It looks big enough to hold a person. Even a tallish one, like me. My mind goes temporarily blank as I face the reality that I am most likely going to die today.

Will I sing in my own death? Is that a thing, for banshees?

No amount of lip-biting or hand clutching can now hide the tremors that rush through my body in waves. For some reason, at the moment of facing my coming death, my mind suddenly kick-starts out of its terror-induced lethargy, filling with thoughts of the sexy winter warrior.

Tarrien, I wish we could have gotten to know each other properly. I wish we'd had more time.

I lock my knees, determined not to collapse in a puddle of fear in front of these hideous creatures. The robed man still standing behind me pushes me between the shoulder blades, urging me forward.

I can't do this. I can't be here in this place. So much death.

I turn and punch the man in the face. He staggers back, bringing his hands to his already-bleeding nose, and the distraction provides an opening to flee.

Somewhere in the back of my mind I realized the chanting has stopped, which means all eyes are likely on me. *Run!* I race toward the door but have only taken a few steps when a clutch of magic grabs at me. The enchantment renders me immobile. I growl, trying to push the magic off me and away, force the grip that holds me to let go. Whoever has me is far too strong.

Oily tendrils, visible even to my eyes, wrap around

me. I find myself lifted high into the air, coaxed forward to levitate over the heads of the avidly watching crowd below, until I hover horizontally above the altar slab. The magic squeezes so tight I can barely breathe.

I'm not sure which is worse: the lack of air, or the feeling of utter helplessness at being restrained in this way.

Who has me in their grip? A slight lessening of the pressure around my throat enables me to turn my head to the side and my heart sinks when I notice what I hadn't seen before.

There is a raised dais behind the altar. On the dais rests a throne-like chair, currently occupied by the exiled fae queen. She stares at me with her sweet glamor finally stripped away completely. All the innate darkness within her is now resident on her features.

She is evil, through and through. No doubt whatsoever is left in my mind as I stare back into those malevolent eyes.

But even the queen can't hold my attention for more than a few seconds. Not when I notice the male who is standing behind her, almost hidden in the shadows. Like the others around the fire pit, he is wearing a dark robe, and with his long dark hair loose, he blends in to the shadowy background in a way that encourages my eyes to miss his presence altogether.

Only I can't miss him—not when he has one arm held out toward me like that, with his hand in a claw shape directing an oozing purple miasma straight at me.

The magic is there, but not quite there, almost like heat waves rising from tarmac. He's the one holding me immobile. All by himself. Which makes him a powerful threat in his own right.

And yet, I don't think he is a necromancer, even though he is clearly channelling purple wizard magic. He has an otherworldly air about him, that reminds me of the queen. I think this man might be fae. As if he hears my thoughts, he shakes his head, shifting his hair backward. The action reveals his pointy ears and confirms my guess.

Who is he? Silver-gray eyes regard me steadily, and my heart flip-flops unevenly in my chest. It can't be. Those eyes...

It can't possibly be.

I swallow hard and force out the question. "Tarrien?"

Even as I say his name, I realize I must be wrong. There is no way the winter warrior would be involved in something as evil as this. He might be annoying, and need some lessons in relationship skills, but Tarrien has a brave and decent heart. I know it, with every fiber of my being.

I squint into the shadows, trying to ascertain who it might be.

This is a slightly older fae. I notice a few strands of gray in the dark hair and he has a slightly less muscled presence than the winter warrior I was wrapped around in bed only a few short days ago. Despite the physical differences, and the misleading shadows that make it hard to see anything, the resemblance is clear enough.

"You're his father, aren't you?" I say. "The one who betrayed them all, with *her*."

The shadows increase around the figure, swirling until I can barely see him at all.

"Coward," I spit out. "Hiding in the shadows behind the ex-queen. Why not step out and own what you did?"

They're going to kill me anyway, I figure, so it doesn't really matter what I say, now. I'm still looking at Tarrien's dad as I speak—or at least, in his general direction, now that he's almost completely hidden—but the queen hisses between her teeth. She really didn't like that ex-queen jibe. I've probably just escalated my coming torture and death.

I search through the shadows for one final shot at the fae man. All I can see now is that damn, clawed hand. "Tarrien has been sworn to protect me, you know. And he'll find me and kill your merry little band of perverted followers. I have total faith in your son."

A titter of crazed laughter from some of the robed figures in the room seems to break through the temporary stand-off. Tarrien's father straightens his fingers and withdraws his hand back into the shadows. I drop out of the air unceremoniously onto the slab and all the breath is knocked from my lungs. I gulp and scrabble to get up, until I am held once again in place by that invisible, shadowed claw-hand. The queen rises and steps forward.

She leans over me, her gaze murderous. "Tell us your name, banshee-hybrid, and we will let you live."

Yeah, right. I really believe you, bitch.

The queen gestures someone from the group around the fire to come forward, and I try in vain to scramble away. Tarrien's father remains silent in the darkness behind the queen, presumably the one still holding me in place.

Then the queen does a little hand wave of her own, and a blast of magic hits me in the face. Pain such as I've never felt before almost crushes my head from the outside in. *His* magic already holds me firmly in place. This bonus blast from her is nothing but torture for torture's sake.

I am glued to this damn slab, while suffering the migraine from hell.

I hear pitiful moaning, and realize it's my own voice. The pain is so intense I can't stop keening like a baby. If I ever felt powerless in my life before, this is ten thousand times worse.

After what feels like an eternity, but may only be a few seconds, the pain in my head eases, though I still cannot move.

"Your name?" The queen waits, and I manage a weak grin.

"Indigo."

Her face turns ruddy, and she nods stiffly. "So be it."

A robed man appears in my vision. Oh, great. It's the guy who collected me from the bathing room. The one who enjoyed the view of my privates a little too much. This time, he holds a stiletto-style blade in one hand.

So, this is it? This is the end?

There is something I have to ask before I die. I need to know...

"Did you kill my friend, Sienna?" I direct my gaze past the throne toward the man still wrapped in shadows. "Are you the one responsible for all this... horror? These...abominations?"

A quick flash of white teeth is my answer. He's *smiling*. The fucking bastard. No doubt about who is the true monster in this room.

The queen releases a strange growling sound. Clearly, she doesn't like that my attention has wandered from her. "*I* am in charge here. Not him. You will address *me*."

Well. I amend my thoughts. No doubt about this *pair* of true monsters. They're all monsters, here, but these two? They deserve each other.

As if she hears my judgemental thought and wants to demonstrate its truth, she reaches out and stabs my cheek with one of her long, pointed fingernails. The pain is sharp and unexpected and brings tears to my eyes despite my efforts to control myself.

She raises up her hand. A drop of my blood meanders from her nail tip down her finger. The red color against her pale skin is oddly mesmerizing.

"Beautiful," she says. "Your blood will do nicely."

An appreciative murmur from the crowd reminds me that we have an audience. The queen waves her hand and a pretty white bowl materializes in her upturned palm.

She hands the bowl to stiletto guy. "Cut her, and drain it into this."

Cut me? *Drain* me? Terror builds in my chest and a tiny moan escapes my throat as I strain against the magic holding me rigid. The effort is futile.

She leans over me. "We will take your blood, either way, but provide us with your true name, and we will only need a few drops. You will be allowed to live."

My chin trembles. I clamp my teeth together to try and control the fear and stop myself blurting out the name I can hardly remember. *Indigosturianawella*. That was the tongue-twister moniker my dear mother gave me, for some reason. The word hovers on my lips and I bite down on them to stop it from coming out.

What good will my name do them? Why do they need it so much? And what are they planning to do with my blood? Are they going to drink it? Paint themselves in it? Make a stew with it in that big, black pot bubbling away just out of my line of vision?

And here I was, worrying earlier that this ritual would involve something sexual. Laughter threatens and I know I am close to losing it.

"Choose not to cooperate, little hybrid," the queen continues, "and we will drain you completely. Garner every...last...drop. And then, we will find and drain all your bastard siblings, until there is a river of banshee blood, and their deaths will be your fault, because you didn't give us your name."

The man with the knife moves suddenly and fast, lifting my almost-not-there dress and stabbing hard at my upper thigh.

My thigh? You chose my *thigh*, you fucking pervert? You couldn't have chosen my *wrist*? If my eyes could burn holes through a person, stiletto guy would be swiss cheese right now.

At first, the pain is hardly there at all, just a burning sensation that suddenly grows hotter. Blood begins to seep out of the wound and down my leg into the bowl that the man shoves between my legs.

I can barely move at all. Only my eyes, darting about as I search vainly for any means of escape, and my mouth, twisting in a mix of terror and hatred. And my lungs. At least I can still breathe. For now.

"Give us your name!" The queen's screech fills the air.

The man smirks, and stares down lasciviously at my exposed privates, before bringing the stiletto to his mouth and licking it. For some reason, that action is the very last straw out of all the things I have already endured.

Everything inside me reacts. I open my mouth, and instead of giving them any words, I let loose with the loudest and most haunting banshee song I have ever allowed to cross my lips.

They should never have left me with breath in my lungs.

I give them everything that the theater crowd have always wanted, and far more than any of my human audiences could ever truly take. I sing of death, and life, and all things between. I sing of the moment of extinguishment, the black grief when someone disappears from existence, and the utter joy of new life, of resurrection.

I sing the song of the banshee, and I do not hold back at all.

Chapter Ten

They say the song of the banshee is the most terrifying sound in existence.

Perhaps it is.

The queen staggers away, shrieking and covering her ears. Stiletto guy drops the knife and cowers, hunching until he is out of my view. Beneath the perfect notes releasing from my throat I hear the frightened cries and screams from the crowd who gathered to watch whatever this ritual would have entailed.

Through it all, I stare straight into the shadows at the Tarrien look-alike.

Take that, you murdering bastard. You killed my beautiful friend. Now you can experience the song that I had to sing for her.

He steps out past the throne and I see him clearly for the first time. He grits his teeth and scrunches his face, struggling to hold onto the enchantment freezing me in place.

The banshee song continues to wash over him; over them all. *Dying and death. And life. And then dying once again. And death. Do you like the cycle of existence, father of Tarrien?*

As I reach a crescendo, the magic holding me captive finally collapses into nothing. I've done it. I've broken through his concentration. I launch up onto my bare feet, standing on top of the altar, and continue to power my voice and my song outward. I reach into every nook and cranny of the room, turning in a circle, filling it all with sound.

I ignore the prone and writhing robed figures. They are nothing but followers, pathetic and weak. Instead, I focus on the queen, who has jumped back up onto the dais and reached Tarrien's father. They stand together, in front of that damn throne. Her hands are still over her ears. I step up my attack, sending everything I have in their direction.

The man's face is murderous, and I sense a rolling swell of power at the periphery of my consciousness. I have never felt anything like it before. I know it is coming from him, and I know that the moment my voice falters, he will blast whatever he is holding onto my way. It will crush me. I feel it already, chipping away at the edges of my song, looking for a crack. Waiting.

I can't keep singing. The banshee call is draining me of everything I have...

Is it the banshee call that is causing this feeling of dizziness? I don't usually feel as weak as this when I sing. Not unless death is involved. *My death*? My legs tremble hard, as if no longer able to hold me up. I look down, at a huge pool of blood all over the altar, and realize I've been bleeding out of my thigh wound all this time.

How is that possible? It was only a needle-sized hole. That man must have nicked an artery. I shake my head, blinking. My vision is wonky. Another rush of dizziness sends my head spinning. Blackness threatens at the edges of my vision...

Oh, God. Am I dying? Have they drained me, despite my song? Have I inadvertently drained myself?

As the blackness grows, it becomes harder to focus. My song falters and eventually fails. The wave of magic that had been waiting in the wings rushes over me, but it feels less powerful than before. I guess he must have drawn it back inside himself, saving his energy. He knows I'm so weak from loss of blood that he doesn't need to crush me. I am already done.

As the room falls silent, the queen straightens, her eyes flashing fury and her smile wide and grim. Now there's one who won't hold back. Tarrien's father places a hand on her shoulder, as if in caution. She shakes him off and faces me. Even with my failing vision I read the murderous intent in her expression. She lifts her hand...

And then a flash of bright silver light fills the air.

Did the queen do that? Did Tarrien's dad? Judging by the shock that slackens their features, it would appear not.

Hope sparks in my heart as a whole horde of men, dressed just like Tarrien in his dark winter warrior armor, burst into the room. And there is my Tarrien, in the lead, wielding an enormous silver sword in one hand and a wicked-looking dagger in the other. His face is terrifying, and to me, utterly beautiful.

My Tarrien. I like the sound of that. Is it really him? Or is it my dying brain, conjuring up the one person in the world I most want to see right now? The one person I will most regret not getting to know properly in this lifetime.

Oh, Tarrien. I wish we had the chance of a future, together. I think it would have been magnificent.

Too late. Far too late. My mind is fuzzy and I can't formulate proper thoughts or words. Not anymore.

My song is done.

I collapse onto the bloody slab and warm blackness claims me.

Tarrien

I'VE NEVER in my life seen a more beautiful, nor terrifying, sight, than Indie standing up on that blood-soaked altar in a see-through dress, her lower half covered in blood. Her dark hair streams out as she swivels around to face me.

She's alive. Thank the winter gods. I am not too late.

Our gazes meet for just a moment, and I see relief, and something more, in the depths of her brilliant emerald eyes. I want to explore that *something more*, desperately, but now is not the time.

Her face is so white it scares me. Even her lips are leached of color. My brain suddenly registers how much blood surrounds her on that stone slab. More, perhaps, than a part-fae could stand to lose and still survive. She crumples into a tiny heap amidst the blood.

I release an enraged roar. *No! I will not let them kill her. I will not.*

My bellow echoes throughout the cavernous room and I rush into the throng alongside the warriors who joined me on this mission, swiping left and right and removing necromancer heads as I go.

A row of abominations forms and for the first time I realize this crowd is a mix of wizards, a couple of witches, and warped supernaturals. I pause to count the row facing us. Seven vamps and seven werewolf loups. I point some of my warriors toward a few of the robed necromancers still alive who are scrabbling for the exit, and the remaining five warriors automatically form a line behind me.

Six of us, against fourteen of them. Not impossible, though we need to do this fast, or Indie will not live.

The loups all rush us at the same time, and the sounds of battle fill the air once again. Screams and cries, and metal against bone. Growling and hissing and yelling, and gurgles as some of them die, choking on their own foul blood.

Too late I remember Indie's banshee magic, amongst all this death and dying. Will she survive that on top of what they've done to her, if she is already so weak?

I shoot a glance toward the altar. She isn't moving at all, and has not made a single sound as all these creatures die around her. That is unheard of for a banshee. Unless the banshee in question is dead.

I hope she is merely unconscious, and not... *No. Focus.* I can battle and heal at the same time, as long as I maintain my concentration.

I send a swirl of healing magic toward her, praying it will be enough to hold her until I can get her back to Faerie and repair the damage properly. I cannot do more than that with a were's jaws threatening to close on my throat and a vamp on my back dragging at my head to assist the were.

I crash deliberately backward onto the ground, a surprised squeal released in my ear by the vamp as my weight combined with my armor crushes the creature enough to force it to let go. Its spindly hold releases and it wriggles out from beneath me and jumps away. I jab up and into the were's chest with my dagger. Silver, with a wooden core. Perfect for felling any of these creatures. Any, except fae.

The were collapses onto me as it dies, so close to my face that its death gurgle fills my lungs with its fetid breath. I cough to rid myself of the putrid stench, and then breathe shallowly under the weight of the furry body until I manage to shove it off me.

As I do, I notice a sparkle of something metal at its neck. A medallion, with a strange swirling design. I remember Indie's sister asking me if I had seen something like this. Guided by instinct, I conjure a handkerchief, and then for good measure, a sealed plastic bag. I use the handkerchief to rip the necklace off the dead were, and then fold it into the linen wrap and seal it into the bag. I tuck the package into my boot to consider later, before jumping to my feet, checking out the rest of the room. My fellow warriors—assembled at a moment's notice back in Faerie when I sent out the call—are gaining the upper hand over the remaining abominations.

There don't appear to be any necromancers left alive.

I turn my attention to the fae woman standing on the dais behind the altar. *My queen. Or rather, my ex-queen.*

Indie's folded up body between us looks tiny and helpless. She is so still and pale. Too still. Too pale.

I direct another wave of healing magic Indie's way, the tentacles reaching out from deep within me to wrap her and hold her tight. I can sense her essence, still hanging on, within the cradle of my magical embrace. She may not be conscious, but she is definitely still alive—at least for now.

Hold on, my love. I will get you home as soon as I am able.

I rush toward the altar, judging the distance and the height, and take a giant leap over the top of the stone slab. I land on my feet near the throne. Rhiannon takes a few small steps backward, away from me.

There was someone standing with her when we first arrived in the room. I caught the flash of a tall male lurking in the shadows behind Rhiannon. My momentary lapse of attention when I saw the spectacle of Indie—my beautiful, brave Indie—standing up on that slab and facing her enemies like an amazing Valkyrie warrior, gave whoever it was the opportunity to disappear.

No matter. I am positive I know who it was. And he will not get away with this. I will make sure of it.

I have to restrain myself from launching at Rhiannon and grabbing her around the neck. Even if she were to use her magic against me, my wrath is such that I would likely squeeze the life out of her before I could gather any useful information.

I narrow my gaze and glare at her. My control is balanced on a dagger's edge. She must sense how close I am to snapping, because she sucks in a ragged breath and takes yet another step back.

"Time to end this, Rhiannon." I can barely force the words past the constriction in my throat.

She holds out her hands in a beseeching manner. "You could join our cause, Tarrien. The Restoration Movement offers rewards beyond anything you have ever imagined. I would never have you working as a lackey, a glorified security guard. The way Renna has treated you since I left the Winter Court is disgraceful. You deserve so much more."

The fact that I agree with her about Renna is moot. "I think not. It's over, Rhiannon. Give yourself up now, to my warriors, and I will guarantee you maintain your dignity, at least."

I will ensure Rhiannon dies for what she has done. But not here, and not now. We need to extract as much information as we can. If I act now, in this moment, we may never discover the full extent of her plan, nor identify all her allies. More innocent victims might die. We need that information from her, to rid both the mortal and fae worlds of the rot that has permeated everything, almost since the Accord began.

The Restoration Movement, she just called it. At least now, we have a name for the enemy.

"If you take me back now, you and I both know what will happen, Tarrien," she says in a pleading tone. Her eyes are calculating, though. Their coldness does not match her beseeching voice, and I do not trust her at all. Especially not when her hands are tucked behind her back, potentially concocting a magical attack.

"King Tryppton loved you, once," I say. "He will—"

"Tryppton will torture me, and then kill me, and he'll enjoy doing it. Please don't send me back."

She's not wrong. The king will indeed be most pleased to receive this prisoner in the dungeons of the Winter Palace, and her stay will not be pleasant. Unfortunately for Rhiannon, I have nothing but loathing in my heart for her. She should never have tried to kill Indie.

I reach behind me with my awareness, through the tentacles connecting me to my banshee. I confirm she is still alive, though barely. For the first time, doubt at my own ability both to battle and heal creeps in. What if I'm too late? What if *this*—I blast more power through the strands—is not enough?

I need to get her back to my quarters and locate all the strands that connect her to this life. I need to rebuild some of them and strengthen others, in order to bring her back whole.

I gesture to two of the warriors to come forward, providing quick instructions for transporting the queen back to Faerie's Winter Court. They will temporarily freeze the captor, which will hold her magic in stasis and effectively renders her powerless.

Rhiannon's lip curls up in a sneer as the warriors approach. Her hands are still tucked behind her. I watch carefully, waiting for whatever magic onslaught she might send our way.

"Rhiannon," I start to say. "You—"

"That's *Queen* Rhiannon to you, Tarrien."

She quickly thrusts her arms and a ball of silver attack magic launches at the warriors. I jump to deflect it with my sword, and draw my short dagger.

"You're not a queen. You're nobody's queen, anymore. Remember?"

Her eyes flash with rage. "When I am reinstated, I will remember those who supported me, and those who did not."

"Those who supported you? Like my father, you mean?"

Her gaze flickers over her shoulder toward the shadows, and then back to me, confirming my guess. It *was* him. Sadness touches my heart and I realize I was holding out hope that my father had not fully crossed over to the dark side. Futile to hope for something I already knew was untrue.

"I will hunt him down, and I will kill him, you know," I say. "Just like I will kill *you*, Rhiannon, once the king has extracted the information he needs. For what you both have done to so many, and for what you in particular have done to..."

I swallow back her name. I will not let this fae bitch see that the ice around my own warrior heart has the capacity to melt, and reform, and melt again.

She narrows her eyes. "What I have done to... Indigo? Ah, Tarrien. Poor little warrior boy. So, you *are* just like your father underneath that impressive armor. Only..." She glances past me, over my shoulder. "You are too late to save your little banshee. She is too far gone. In fact, I think she is already dead. Pity."

Dead? *She can't be. I'm keeping her alive.* Even though I still feel Indie's essence, I can't help the glance back at her. The queen hurls another ball of magic and this time it hits me directly in the face and bounces off to hit the other two warriors.

Silver blasts all around us and my vision disappears. I slash with my sword and my dagger where she stood, the blades finding nothing. I already know what I will find when the silver mist clears.

She is gone. My father is gone. And I am left with a whole room full of dead abominations and necromancers.

Plus, the woman who managed to melt the ice around my heart without me even realizing. I sprint the short distance back to Indie, all the while barking instructions at the remaining warriors to stay and clean up the mess in this forsaken place.

Gently, I lift her up into my arms. "Indie. I've got you, now."

She is floppy and non-responsive. Is the queen

correct? Have I dallied too long, trying to be a hero and capture Rhiannon?

Self-disgust fills me. I should have taken Indie home immediately, instead of assuming I had the strength and expertise to battle and heal at the same time. Why did I not leave this battle to the others? Why did I not take her out of here the second I arrived?

"Hold on, my love. Stay with me."

If she has already begun to cross over into oblivion, then nothing I do will be enough. There is no amount of winter warrior healing magic strong enough to bring her back, if she has already passed out of this plane of existence.

Chapter Eleven

INDIGO

It's the warmth that seeps in first. Delicious warmth, and the feeling of being safe and comforted in loving arms. I smile and stretch, wondering how I could possibly have slept so long and so dreamlessly that I can't even remember the night before. I can't even remember...

My eyelids pop open. I sit bolt upright, then grab my head as a wave of dizziness washes over me. I fall back into the pillows and groan. What the hell did I do last night? How much did I have to drink?

Awareness that this is not my own bed arrives slowly, and as it does, patches of memory begin to return. The ritual. All those leering faces. The pure evil leaching from that hideous fae queen.

This time I sit up with a bit more decorum, and the dizziness stays away. I'm in a bedroom, quite sparsely furnished with only the bed I'm lying in, a side table, a wardrobe tucked in the corner of the room, and a couple of chairs set on a rug in front of a small fireplace. The sparse nature of it all should be unpleasant, but it is not. Instead, there's a warm and cozy feel to the space, which is enhanced by the lit fire in the grate. The flames provide a gentle golden glow in addition to several lit sconces dotted around the stone walls.

The bed itself is huge, constructed of wood and with a silver-gray quilt covering my lower half. It is the most comfortable bed I've ever been in, and the feeling of warmth and security stays with me, even though I'm now sitting up.

"Where am I?"

A slight chuckle to my left has my head turning, and I realize Tarrien is kneeling by the bed. He looks exhausted. He is strained around the eyes, and there are lines at the sides of his mouth that I don't remember being there before.

I want to reach up and caress him, but my hand closest to him is clasped in one of his. I become aware that the sense of security emanates from our connection. I regard our clasped fingers and decide to leave my hand resting in his.

"Welcome back, Indie," he says. "You're in my bed. In Faerie."

"Am I? But..." I frown, staring around. "Aren't you from the Winter Court? I imagined something different to this. All, I don't know, ice and coldness.

This is...lovely. Homely." I glance at the fireplace. "Won't the fire melt things?"

This time his laugh is full-throated.

"I do hail from the Winter Court, which is where we are now, and there is quite a bit of snow and ice outside. Inside, our homes are whatever we want them to be. And I enjoy an open fire, much of the time. It hasn't melted anything in the past few hundred years, so I'm sure we'll be fine."

His expression changes from lightly amused to serious. "Which brings me to you. How do you feel, Indie? Are you...fine?"

At his words, the whole slew of memory comes rushing back in then, not just in patches this time. *So much blood. So much terror.*

I shudder and rip my hand out of Tarrien's, before reaching down under the covers with my free hand, exploring my thigh. The wound has disappeared, and I feel...*well*. There's no other word to describe the sense of physical well-being. My mental well-being, on the other hand, may take a while to recover.

"They drained my blood. Didn't they? I don't think I should feel this well after...after..."

I can't finish. Tears prick at my eyes and I bite my lip, trying to use willpower to hold them in. Tarrien jumps up from his position on the floor and sits on the edge of the bed. His white shirt and dark trousers show off his muscled physique. In this ordinary-looking bedroom setting, I could almost imagine we are two normal human beings, in the human world, in the tentative early stages of a developing relationship. No fae magic, or madness, or evil creatures running around trying to kill me. I stifle a laugh before it turns into a sob.

"It's okay, Indie. You're safe. I promise you, no one is going to hurt you, here."

"I know. I..." I fold my arms across my belly, clutching my elbows.

He tentatively places his arm across my shoulders and draws me in to his side. His delicious scent rises around me, causing butterflies in my belly. I allow the embrace, leaning into him. His body emits warmth and I crave warmth. I crave *his* warmth in particular. Which sounds ridiculous, given he's a winter fae. And yet, here we are in Winter Faerie, and I'm being warmed by an open fire and a fae warrior who is hot in every sense of the word.

"Are all winter fae as warm as you?" I ask.

"Winter fae vary a lot. Some are warm, and others —like winter warriors—carry the power of ice permanently within our veins. The connection with winter is supposed to keep us focused on our role as protector." He lifts his shoulders in a slight shrug. "Though, for some reason, it does seem as though your presence heats me up, more than the norm."

"Oh." A small smile plays on my lips. "I don't know if that's a good or a bad thing from your point of view. But I have to admit, I kind of like that idea, actually."

His arm tightens around me. "Several days ago, I'd have insisted it was a very bad thing for a winter warrior. Now..."

He pauses, and I tilt up my head to stare at him.

"Now?" I prompt, when he doesn't speak.

He meets my gaze squarely. "Now, I very much like that idea, too."

This close, I see the interesting flecks of silver that decorate the gray of his irises. The color is entrancing, and draws me in until my breath hitches and I can't think straight.

Last time I saw Tarrien, he was wearing dark fae armor and waving a sword in the air, his eyes flashing silver and the promise of death etched across his features. He should have been terrifying. He *was* terrifying. But he was also magnificent. A true hero riding to my rescue.

Right now, he seems much more approachable, though no less magnificent. My pulse rate begins to speed up.

"It *was* definitely you, who came to rescue me? I didn't imagine that?"

"Of course, it was me." His voice is slightly indignant.

My tense muscles relax at the tone. He has an ego, though I'm willing to forgive that given the kindness and courage he has displayed toward me.

"Though when we arrived," he says, "it looked like

you were doing a damn good job of holding them off all by yourself, little banshee."

"Hmm." I try to laugh but it comes out sounding a bit pathetic. "I was pretty much all out of banshee song. Good thing you appeared when you did. I was down to a pathetic little squeak."

He squeezes me super-tight for a moment, as if he knows how much effort it is taking for me to try and keep things light. "In some ways I'm glad you passed out, Indie. There was a lot of death in that room. I would not have wanted to put your banshee half through that horror and carnage."

This time my chuckle is slightly more genuine. "A positive from a negative, then. Though I have to admit, I honestly didn't expect to survive. How *did* I survive? I think I lost a lot of blood back there in...where was I held, Tarrien?"

His expression turns grave. "You were in a place known as the Badlands. It hovers on the edge of the fae realm, almost in the human realm but not quite. It is neither one place nor the other. Right at the edge of The Nothing."

Badlands. That sounds pretty much on a par with what it felt like to be there. And at the edge of nothing? I shudder and turn my face into Tarrien's chest. His scent rises, subtle and comforting.

"Did you use your winter warrior skills and heal me?"

"I did."

How can a man have two such contrasting sides? A warrior, and a healer. Someone who forges into battle seemingly without fear, slashing and chopping and killing without mercy, and then in the next instant he can turn around and be the complete opposite: a healer who can bring life back to those who hover on the edge of death.

In some ways, he reminds me of my own banshee side. The song of death is also the song of life; of new beginnings. Two opposing yet complementary sides. One cannot exist without the other.

Tarrien fascinates me in a way no one ever has before.

I realize he is still speaking, and tune back in. "It was touch and go, for a while. You were right. You had lost a *lot* of blood, Indie. Far too much. For a few minutes there..."

His voice trails off and I tilt my head back so I can study his face again. His mouth is a grim line and his features communicate guilt as well as tiredness. What on earth does he have to be guilty about?

"I thought I'd delayed too long. I cast strands to begin the healing process while I battled there in the Badlands, but even so, I parried insults with Rhiannon when I should have focusing purely on you." He shakes his head, not trying to hide his self-disgust.

"I don't remember."

"No, you wouldn't. You were not even partly conscious, by the time I brought you back here. I thought I wasn't going to be strong enough to retrieve all the strands that keep you connected to life. I thought I'd failed you."

Pain flashes in his eyes, and I pat him gently on the chest.

"But you didn't. And you were strong enough." I wriggle a bit, stretching my arms and legs and experimenting to see the extent of my physical state. "See? I'm all fixed. You should cut yourself some slack, Tarrien."

"Slack?"

"You know, rope. It's...oh, never mind. Just focus on the fact that I'm here and I'm fine, and it's all thanks to you."

He removes his arm from my shoulders, and runs his hands through his hair. For the first time since we met, he looks rather dishevelled. It does nothing to lessen his overall sexiness. My woman bits choose this moment to wake up. I try to ignore the ache of desire between my legs, and move a lock of hair away from where it has fallen across his cheek.

"How long have I been out of it, Tarrien?"

"A day and a half since I brought you back here."

"Have you had any rest in that time?"

"No. At first I was working to bring you back, and then... well." His cheeks darken in a slight blush. My brows rise at the sight.

"And then?" I prompt.

"And then, once you moved out of danger into a

more natural state, I just enjoyed watching you sleep. That probably sounds creepy to you, right?"

A chuckle bursts out of me. "No creepier than finding out you'd been stalking around spying on me for a week, when I didn't know you were there."

"Indie, I apologize for—"

"Stop apologizing. I'm teasing you, Tarrien. You know, if we are going to spend time together, then I think we're going to have to extend that sense of humor of yours."

"I want to spend time with you, and I would not want anyone else teaching me how to be less serious. But there's something you should know...something I should have told you straight away..."

I sigh, perhaps a little more dramatically than I need to, but he doesn't take the hint. Seems like "serious" Tarrien is still in play.

"I couldn't sense where you were straight away, when they first snatched you from the club," he says. There is a note of apology in his tone. "It wasn't me who located you in the Badlands, Indie. It was Renna. *Renna*, of all people! Once she did, I was able to home in on your essence, but you have your mother to thank for finding you in the first place."

"Renna? *She* helped find me?"

He nods. "If I had located you sooner, then maybe you wouldn't have been traumatized, or hurt. It's my fault you almost—"

"Stop! None of this is your fault. It's that goddamn

exiled stupid fucking queen of yours." I frown. "Our queen, I guess, if you count a half-fae as one of your own. And…"

Here's the tricky bit. I don't quite know how to raise this with Tarrien. There's simply no easy way to say it. In the end, I take a deep breath and blurt it out.

"The person helping her with her evil plan might have been related to…you. I think—well, actually, I don't think, I *know*—it was…your father. He looked almost exactly like you, and given what you told me about his relationship with the banished queen… well…" I shrug, not needing to say more.

There. That was gentle enough, wasn't it?

Tarrien stands and begins to pace back and forth across the room. His distress is evident in the jerky movements and the grim set of his features.

Hmm. Maybe not gentle enough.

"I'm sorry," I add. "I didn't mean to—"

"It's fine, Indie. I know my father is involved. The queen as much as confirmed it, before she escaped. I always suspected, which is why I've continued to do Renna's bidding for so long. Trying to make amends, in my own way, for something I always felt guilty about on my family's behalf."

My heart squeezes tight when I see his anguish and I wish I could tell him otherwise. But he deserves to know the truth.

"He *was* there, Tarrien, and I don't think he was helping her, as such. I think he was in control of them all. Even the queen, though she wants everyone to believe she's in charge. He—your father—might be the actual mastermind behind all of this...horror."

"I didn't know for sure, Indie."

"I know you didn't."

"Not until I burst into that ritual and saw Rhiannon standing behind you. *She* almost brought down the Winter Court with her betrayal and her hunger for power." He finally stops pacing and turns to face me, his eyes steely gray.

"But *he* is the one who creates and controls those abominations. Not her. *He* did it. And I will do everything in my power to stop him. I don't care what it takes. The day my father chose evil over good, is the day he ceased to be my blood."

I don't know what drives me, other than instinct. I throw back the bed covers and jump out, rushing over to Tarrien and sliding my arms around his waist.

After a moment, his arms come around me, too. The embrace feels right, and I don't want to let him go.

Eventually, I realize that I'm wearing a white nightdress, and no underwear. None whatsoever.

"Umm, what happened to that dress I had on when you rescued me?" I ask.

He wrinkles his nose. "That blood-soaked piece of fabric that barely covered anything, even though it reached your feet? I had it burned."

"Oh. Good. But..." I swallow nervously. "Who undressed me, when I got here?"

"I did." His brows rise up as he stares down at me. "I don't understand. Is that an issue? I've seen it all before, remember?"

Oh, yes, I remember.

My cheeks begin to heat, as do other parts of me.

"I don't have an issue with that," I say, my husky voice already communicating my growing need.

Tarrien crushes me against him, leaving me in no doubt whatsoever about his need being very much in sync with mine. His flesh is firm against my belly.

I release a shaky breath, and stand on my tiptoes to receive his kiss. The added height brings his organ into contact with my aching clit instead of my belly, and I release a moan that disappears into Tarrien just as his mouth connects with mine.

His answering groan is deep and rough as we press against each other. The sound reverberates all the way through me. My lips explore his with abandon, and he deepens the kiss as our tongues slip and slide and dance with each other in an erotic parody of actual lovemaking.

When we finally break apart, we are both breathing fast. There are spots of color in Tarrien's cheeks, and I'm sure my own face is equally flushed.

"Can you do that thing again, the trick with the disappearing clothing?" I can hardly speak, due to the waves of desire that wash over me.

"Hmm. That's a big ask, Indie, considering how much clothing you have on."

A bubble of laughter pops out of me. "I guess you've passed your first lesson in humor with flying colors."

He does a little wave with one of his hands, and we are both instantly naked. His skin against mine is warm and smooth, and I run my hands appreciatively over his chest and across his shoulders.

One of his hands cups a breast. "I believe I am a quick learner, Indie."

His mouth descends and he draws in a nipple, sucking and licking so deeply that I feel the pull all the way down in my womb.

"Oh, I think you must be. That feels so good," I gasp.

He raises his head and stares at me, his eyes all silver. No gray whatsoever.

"That is only the beginning of the onslaught, Indie."

When he places his hands on my buttocks and lifts me up, I wrap my legs around his hips. He kisses me again, and carries me back to the bed. He lays me on my back and then kneels on the floor between my open legs.

"I hope *this* feels even better." He dips his head between my legs, and takes my clit into his mouth, licking and sucking until I can't think at all, but only feel. The sensation is so intense I moan and buck beneath him, the pressure building to an intensity that is beyond anything I have ever experienced.

"Tarrien, I can't hold on. I'm going to...please, I need you inside me..."

He is up in a flash, onto the bed, and he settles his rigid flesh right at the entrance to my channel. Everything down there is slick and wet from his mouth, and when I lift my hips to meet him, the head of his cock slides in without any resistance whatsoever.

He grunts, and thrusts hard, seating himself fully inside me. Again, I wrap my legs around his hips and buttocks. The feel of his fullness within and the weight of him on my outer sex are like twin pressures that are exquisite and almost unbearable.

He balances on his elbows and stares down at me. "When I was healing you, Indie, I had to dig deep inside to find your essence."

"Really?" I jiggle my hips, reminding him to move.

Instead, his hips remain still. He bends his head and kisses me so gently on the lips that the connection is almost not there. But the effect is so intense it takes me right to the edge of the precipice. If he moves now, I will explode around him in a violent orgasm.

"I found your banshee essence, Indie. Deep down inside you. I found your life threads, but I also found your death magic."

Before I can react in any way, he breaks out into the biggest smile I have ever seen on his face. The smile creates joy in my heart.

"It was beautiful, Indie. So beautiful. When I bound myself to you, to bring you back, I experienced something I have never before experienced, ever, in my life."

He stares down at me in wonder, and I reach up and cup his cheek.

"You weren't afraid? Death is terrifying, to most. Even to me, sometimes."

"I felt like I had found my soul mate, Indie. I felt like I had found my other half."

With that, he begins to thrust, gently at first and then faster, pounding into me so hard that my head bumps against the headboard.

I don't care. The connection is perfect. He saw my banshee power and he wasn't afraid. He saw me—the *real* me—and it didn't scare him away. The rush of desire is so sudden and explosive, the sensation building so quickly, that I tip over the precipice within seconds, falling into the most intense orgasm of my life.

He releases a guttural roar and follows me into climax, his hot seed rushing into me and our bodies bucking and shuddering together.

As we slowly come back to the moment, the enormity of what he said overwhelms me. I begin to tremble, and the urge to cry becomes so strong I close my eyes tight to contain the emotion.

"What is it, my love?" He presses gentle kisses on my eyelids, and I squeeze them even tighter shut for a moment, before opening my eyes and facing him.

"What you said, about seeing my death magic. The source of my banshee power."

"Yes. Is it okay that I told you? Does it make you... uncomfortable, to have had me poking around inside you?"

Even now, he is doubtful.

"You saved my life, Tarrien. I will be forever grateful for that. It's definitely not that worrying me." I frown, trying to find the right words. "If *you* found my banshee song, then maybe others can find it, too. The queen—"

"Try not to think of her, Indie. She will never again be a threat to you. I promise."

"But it was so awful, Tarrien. They said they would drain me. If I gave them my name, apparently that would amplify the power in my blood, so they wouldn't need to take as much. But I wouldn't give it to them. I knew it wouldn't make any difference to me. I figured I was gonna be dead anyway. But I was hoping it might make a difference to others."

A particular memory rises and I gasp. "She said she's going after my siblings. She's going to drain them all. Because I didn't give them my name. And if she does, then it will be all my fault."

Chapter Twelve

I can't hold in the tears any longer. I hate that I'm crying in front of anyone, but particularly in front of him. I want him to see me as strong and independent.

But I can't help it. I was so afraid, when they took me, and I tried so hard not to let them see it. Now that I'm safe, it seems ridiculous that I can't stop the tears from flowing.

Tarrien, to his credit, doesn't pull away. Instead, he wraps his arms tightly around me and croons in that delightfully soothing tone, in a language I don't understand, until eventually, the tears and the hiccups subside.

"How do you do that?" I hiccup. Okay, maybe not all of them have subsided. "Healing magic?"

"Not healing magic. I don't know. I just hold you, and I feel things. Things I've never felt before. Things I was always told a winter warrior could—or *should*— never feel." He shrugs, still wrapped around me, and I shift until his heart is beneath my ear.

It is beating quite fast, and sounds healthy, for a heart that is meant to be encased in ice.

"And then I tell you about what I'm feeling, in my own language," he adds.

I start to speak—to tell him I want to learn his beautiful language—but my nose is still running. I sniff and stare around in vain for a box of tissues. "What do fae use to blow their noses with?"

His body shakes. I realize he's laughing.

"Now, that is where magic does come in handy. Here." He disentangles himself from me and cradles my face in his hands. Warmth suffuses me, and suddenly my nose is no longer in need of a tissue.

"All fixed?" He places a gentle kiss on the tip of my nose, then moves up to do the same on my forehead.

"Yes. All fixed."

How is it possible that a light kiss can send tremors right through my system, so soon after we sated our desire?

As if he senses my need, his pupils flare, and just like that, desire is re-ignited.

"Will you teach me your language, Tarrien?" My voice is husky.

He smooths back my hair.

"Afterward," he says, and I'm gratified to note his voice is equally as rough.

"After what?" I begin tracing a pattern on his bare chest, aimlessly at first and then with more intent. I swirl downward, until finally I reach the nest of hair at the base of his shaft.

He shudders and releases a tiny groan. "After...oh, that is very nice, Indie. Very nice indeed."

"After...?" I run a fingertip up his shaft, circling the head of his organ. He sucks in his breath.

"After we make love once again," he says in a rush, and flops backward onto the bedcovers. His organ reaches skyward as I continue to circle the tip.

"Only once?" I love teasing him like this. I feel powerful and wanted. I take his shaft in my fist and pump the flesh a few times, enjoying the uneven harshness of his breath.

His hand comes down to cover mine. "Many times, Indie. Perhaps a lifetime's worth of making love. If that appeals to you, of course?"

If that appeals...?

I bend down, sliding him deep into my mouth and throat. I add in my fingers for good measure, cupping his balls and dipping into that little gap behind them that is so sensitive in men. He growls somewhere far above me, his whole body shuddering now.

"For the love of the winter gods, Indie, I need to be inside you. I mean...inside your..."

His voice trails off as I continue to bend and dip and suck, increasing the tempo until the slick burst of flavor in my mouth signals he is fast approaching a climax. I let him free, and then climb over him until I straddle his hips, my pussy hovering just above his rigid organ.

"A lifetime's worth...of this?" I slowly descend, letting his organ slide deep into my channel. I settle myself more comfortably atop him, the pressure inside an exquisite torture that I want to prolong for as long as I can.

He nods frantically in response to my question, seemingly unable to formulate actual words.

"Then yes, please, Tarrien. Making love to you, over and over, appeals to me very much. Far more than I ever expected it to."

I begin to rock back and forth, feeling the increasing pressure in my clit, coupled with additional pressure deep within my belly. The feeling grows, until there is nothing left but Tarrien and me, connected in the most intimate way possible.

When he arches his back and roars, I join him, screaming, and we climax together as he releases his load inside me with a shudder. Endless waves of pleasure engulf my whole body. I collapse against his chest, feeling both shattered, and completed. I cannot understand why this man is the right one for me. But everything—my gut, my heart, and even my head— tells me he is.

When eventually, my heart rate slows to a more normal level and my breathing becomes less ragged, I smile against his chest. I am more replete than I have ever been in my life.

And I couldn't imagine a better place to fall asleep than right here in Faerie, wrapped in Tarrien's muscled arms.

Tarrien

WE BOTH DRIFT in and out of sleep. I have never felt so sated, nor so complete. Even as I slide back into slumber, I know my face is sporting a wide grin.

"Uh, Tarrien?"

Indie's voice seeps into my half-dreams. Dreams where I lay entwined with the woman I love, warm and secure in her embrace. Dreams where I tell her how much I love her, and she says exactly the same in return, and the world does not end, or implode, and nothing evil happens at all. Instead, we decide to stay like this forever, wrapped in each other arms, drawing comfort and strength from one another, two halves of the same soul...complete at last...

"Please wake up, Tarrien. I have something important to ask you."

I blink and come back to consciousness slowly. Indie slips out of my hold and sits up. She brings her knees up to her chest and hugs them. Her skin is so pale and smooth. She's beautiful.

I reach out and caress her arm, enjoying the goosebumps that raise themselves beneath my touch. "What is it, my sexy little banshee?"

A smile lifts her beautiful mouth, though only for a moment. Then a frown descends as she turns to study me and I sense her mood change. I stop touching her and roll properly onto my side, propping myself up on an elbow.

"What is it?" I ask again, this time in a firm tone that shows her I'm genuinely listening.

"I want to find my siblings. Warn them, if I can."

My brows lift. "*All* of them?"

That's potentially a big damn job.

"Well, I don't know exactly how many there are, but I guess Renna can advise us about that. At the very least, I'd like to meet Aleah to start with, and perhaps the SUDAP officer, Maewen, even though, to be honest, she seems quite fierce and scares me a little. I want to warn them about the queen. That bitch is crazy, Tarrien, and I think she was serious about the threat to drain them all. Will you...will you help me?"

"Of course. You're stuck with me now, whether you like it or not, you know."

She rubs her eyes as if exhausted, but her mouth lifts in another grin, and when she drops her hands and looks at me, I read so much in the depths of her beautiful green gaze. The promise of tomorrow—of a future filled with love—is there for my taking, if I'm game enough. *Am I game enough*? I have always prided myself on my brave, emotionless warrior heart, until I met Indie and realized my heart had hardly ever been in use at all.

"Maybe it's the other way round," she teases. "Maybe you're now stuck with *me*. And Lola."

"Good. I like Lola."

"Just as well."

The comment reminds me of something I should have told her earlier. "Um, so, Lola is here."

"What do you mean here? In *Faerie*?"

"Yep. And luckily, she survived the transfer between realms."

"Are you fucking kidding me?" She punches me in the arm. "How could you risk her life like that? I told you not to—"

"I didn't."

"Oh. Well, who did?"

"Your mother. She showed up while you were still unconscious, with your cat under her arm."

She flops back onto the pillows and rolls her eyes. "Of course, she did."

"As much as Renna annoys me," I admit, "I think she was trying to do something kind for you. So, please, don't blame her too much."

Indie sighs. "I won't. As long as Lola's okay." She sits up again. "She *is* okay, right? Where is she?"

I nod. "She's fine. I settled her with a fancy fish dinner in my kitchen. She was very relaxed, to be honest, and had a gentle purr going when I left her."

"Okay, that's good."

She seems suddenly a little lost, and I reach out and take her hands in mine.

"You—and Lola, of course—never have to be alone again, if you don't want to be, Indie. I will be by your side, forever, if you wish it. I will even leave Faerie and live permanently in the human realm, if that's where *you* prefer to live."

"But your job as a winter warrior..."

A chuckle escapes me. "It's not a job. It's who I am. I was born a winter warrior and that will never change, no matter where I live. The thing is, I don't want to be apart from you, Indie. When I first met you, I was afraid. Afraid of emotion. Afraid that if I let you in to my heart, I would turn out like my father and destroy lives. Ruin my family and our reputation even further. But then I *did* get to know you, and somehow you crept in here anyway..."

I tap my chest, over my heart. "I finally learnt what it is to care for someone. To care for *you*. It is not anything to be afraid of. On the contrary. What happened to my father is down to who he is, not the fact that he happened to fall in love."

Indie nods slowly. "We all make moral choices, and that is definitely down to who we are as people. Love is separate to that, and for those of us lucky enough to find love, we still have moral decisions to make. Believe me when I say you are nothing like your father, Tarrien."

My breath catches in my throat and it is a moment before I can speak. "I hope not. I want to be, well, the best I can be. Not the worst. Like *him*."

She wriggles one hand out of mine and raises it to cup my cheek. "You are the best version of you, Tarrien. As corny as that sounds. And I am beginning to care for you quite a lot. Quite intensely, in fact."

Warmth rushes through me at her words. "You care for me, too?"

"Of course, I do. And, being completely honest here, I know what it's like to be afraid of commitment."

Her fingertips on my jawline are almost hypnotic. I hope she keeps that up for a while.

"I've always been alone," she continues. "Even when I was young and being bandied about from one foster home to another. Especially when I left the foster system early, and joined the chorus in the theater group. I was only sixteen. Oh, I have friends. Good friends like Dreya, and my best friend Sienna, who died at the hands of an abomination—though I didn't know that at the time. I am not alone anymore, not really. And yet, I have steered away from love and relationships, because I was always afraid that if I opened up my heart, no one would...stay."

Renna. My mouth tightens. That woman has so much to answer for, when it comes to her children. How many other hybrids are out there, afraid to love because their mother birthed them and ran off without a second thought?

"I will never leave you." I chuck her under the chin, lifting her face to mine. I hope she can read the sincerity in my gaze, because I have never been more serious about anything. "When I couldn't sense you, Indie, and thought I'd lost you…"

I fold her into my embrace. She sighs and relaxes against me and I wonder at the perfect connection.

"I still don't understand exactly what she wants with banshee hybrid blood," Indie says, her voice slightly muffled against my chest.

"The queen? I assume it is something to do with wanting to be reinstated at Court," I say. "Which will never happen while King Tryppton holds the throne. And given what has happened since her exile… what she and my…"

I stop and cough to clear the sudden lump in my throat. It's still hard to verbalize my father's role in so much devastation over so many years. How many innocent people have those abominations killed? Abominations that *he* created in his warped quest for the queen's love.

"What she and my *father* have done," I continue at last, "the only outcome for them both will be execution. No matter who holds the throne, and no matter how long she waits to enact her evil plan."

Indie reaches out and threads her fingers through mine. "I am sorry, Tarrien. I wish it had not been your father."

My laughter is brief. "As do I!" Suddenly my senses

are on alert. Fae are approaching my suite. "Um, I suggest you get dressed quickly, Indie. We are about to have visitors. Including a royal one, if I'm not mistaken."

"What?" She scrambles out of bed so fast she stumbles. I slide out from under the covers more gracefully and catch her elbow to stop her falling. "Is it..."

Looking at her wild eyes, I realize what she must be thinking. "No, no. It's all good. It's not Rhiannon. She cannot return here to Faerie, my love. Not without the permission of the king. You are safe, I promise you."

"Then who—"

"Prince Rhodri, I believe. King Tryppton's signature is slightly different to the one approaching." I pause, and then add for clarification, "Rhodri is Rhiannon's son."

"Her *son*?"

"He's a good man. We grew up together at Court. He supports his father's position in the parental rift, believe me."

She rushes around the room, searching in vain for something suitable to wear, but suddenly stops. "How on earth do you know he's about to visit?"

"Well, we're not on *earth*, as such, but let's put that aside."

She gapes at me, and I have to bite my cheek to stop from laughing. I had no idea that teasing someone could be so much fun. I wave my hand to draw some modern human clothing into the room and clutch my hands around the bundle.

"Royalty has a particular essence when moving through Faerie. It helps their subjects—such as myself—know when to expect a visit from their leaders." I raise my face and sample the air. "And because I have been indebted to your mother for so long, I am familiar with her unique essence, too. Better make haste, Indie. The prince is being accompanied by your mother. Rhodri and Renna will be here momentarily."

"My mother? Oh, fuck," she says. "I mean... oh, God. *Fuck.*"

She notices the bundle of clothes in my hand at that point. "Are they for me?"

When I hand them over, she holds them up and her eyes widen. Jeans, a white tee-shirt, and the low-heeled boots I saw in her wardrobe when I was last at her apartment.

"What is the matter?"

"You said...royalty. Will these be okay? And, um, underwear?"

"Calm down, Indie. Rhodri is very casual, for a fae royal. And to be honest, I rather like you just as you are. Very...enticing."

Her gaze drops to my cock, which has hardened ever so slightly at the beautiful view of her nakedness. Will I ever be sated in this woman's company? I doubt it. The thought gives me a burst of pleasure that is as unexpected as it is welcome.

"I do believe I guessed correctly in relation to sizing. I am good at that."

"Hmm." Her lips tighten but her eyes are laughing at me. "Just for that, forget the underwear. You can imagine my body, rubbing against the jeans fabric. You'll probably see my nipples harden beneath the tee-shirt material, too, as I imagine your fingers, your lips, and your tongue teasing me into a state of full arousal."

My breath hitches in my throat and my body responds far more quickly than it should, given our recent activity in my bed. My cock rises and the heat in my groin becomes heavy and intense.

"Well," she says. "Let's get dressed, shall we? Your prince, and my mother, will be here soon. Momentarily, I think you said?"

Heat flares in my cheeks. "Minx!"

We both rush to cover our nakedness, and we are only just clothed in time when a loud knock sounds at the door to my suite.

It opens before I can answer it, and Prince Rhodri strides into the room with Renna close behind on his heels. *Thank the winter gods we are out of that bed, and fully clothed.*

"Tarrien, I need you to...oh. I didn't realize you had...company."

Prince Rhodri stares at Indie with undisguised interest. Jealousy rears up in my chest and without thinking, I pull Indie into my side and rest my arm across her shoulders.

Mine.

One of Rhodri's brows rises up, and then he seems to do a double-take, looking from Indie to Renna and back again.

"And you're Renna's daughter, I presume?" The prince clicks his heels together and bows slightly. He should look ridiculous, but instead, the action conveys elegance and grace. Indie seems impressed. I will have to practise that move, when I am on my own.

"One of them," she answers, and his lips quirk.

"Your Royal Highness," I say, nodding respectfully.

Indie glances up at me, and then back at the prince, before mimicking my respectful nod. She has probably never before met any fae royalty, given her life in the human realm. Rhiannon doesn't count. She may have been royalty, once, but she gave up the right to call herself that, when she acted so heinously and was banished.

Renna stares at us both, open-mouthed. It's the first time I've ever seen her speechless, and I enjoy the unusual spectacle for a few seconds before I return her stare with a narrow-eyed one of my own.

I dare you to make a snide comment about Indie and me.

She remains silent and eventually shuts her mouth. Her gaze turns speculative rather than annoyed, and my guard lowers a touch. I hadn't realized I was so nervous about her response, until we were standing face to face like this.

I return my attention to the prince. He is similar in height and build to myself, though perhaps a touch taller. His eyes are a bright blue color, far warmer in tone than his mother's. In looks, he favors his father, dark-haired rather than blonde like Rhiannon. His hair is usually tied back like mine, but today it is dishevelled, falling loose down over his shoulders.

"You're the one they kidnapped?" He directs the question to Indie, and she nods.

"Yes. Um. Sir. My name is Indigo." She flashes a glance at her mother, who smiles with what seems to be genuine liking for her daughter.

I really do not understand Lady Renna at all.

"She never gave up her real name," Renna says to the prince. "I am very proud of her."

I feel rather than see Indie's surprised start.

"Thank you, Mother," she says, and then adds, "I believe I also owe you thanks for locating me in the Badlands. Without your help..." She shudders briefly, and I tighten my hold.

Renna looks smug. "I know. Without my help you would be dead, and I would likely be singing in the deaths of many others. I did well, didn't I?"

I roll my eyes. There's the Renna I know.

Indie stifles a snort as the prince advances closer to us.

"Indigo, your bravery in not giving up your true name is noted and appreciated. Without it, we would all be in a whole world of trouble." He scowls. "Thanks mostly to my mother."

"You know?" I study Rhodri carefully, wondering if he feels the same as I do about Father. Betrayed. Full of disbelief and anger that has nowhere to go.

Rhodri's fists clench at his sides. Yep, that's exactly how I feel. Every time I consider my father's actions in this matter, I want to punch the nearest wall.

"Most certainly, Tarrien. *Your* father and *my* mother..." He runs his hands through his hair, messing up the locks even further. "Gods, how did it come to this, man?"

He strides over to the chairs near the fireplace and flops down onto one of them. The rest of us trail over to stand nearby.

"We have to stop them," he says. "And we have to do it before more people die."

"Agreed, Your Highness," I say.

"Oh, quit that. We played together as children, Tarrien. You know you can call me Rhodri."

"Thank you, Rhodri." I incline my head. "And you're correct. We do need to stop them, before they cause more death and destruction. Renna, we were already planning to seek you out, so it is fortunate you accompanied Rhodri. Indie, why don't you..."

I don't want to speak for her. I suspect she would not like that.

"Mother, I would like your assistance to locate as many of my siblings as I can," she says. "I want to warn them of the danger posed by the qu... I mean..." She swallows the word, obviously trying not to give offense.

"You mean, by the queen." Rhodri sits forward, rubbing his face. "It is fine to say it. I am not a delicate flower and it is the truth, after all."

"Well, yes," Indie says. "By the queen. Or rather, ex-queen."

Renna taps her chin. "I can certainly give you the details of your siblings, Indigo. I may not be the most maternal of creatures, but I do keep track of you all in my own way."

"How many are there, Mother?" Indie asks, curiosity lacing her tone.

"Not counting the one in here," she pats her belly and Indie cringes a little, "there are sixteen of you out there in the human realm."

"Sixteen!" Indie shares a glance with me, rolling her eyes, and I bite the inside of my cheek to avoid laughter. It does not seem like the appropriate time.

"I have an idea." I turn to Indie. "I haven't run this past you, yet."

She smiles and nods, as if to show that she is comfortable with anything I say. I want to hug her for the trust she is placing in me.

Instead, I pull the plastic and linen-wrapped medallion from an inside pocket of my shirt. "I grabbed this off one of the dead weres in the Badlands. I think these medallion necklaces might be how my father is piloting the loups. I know Indie's sister Maewen—"

"Oh, little Maewen! I haven't seen her for such a long time," Renna says. "How is she doing?"

My brows come together as I glare at Renna. "She's doing very well indeed, no thanks to you. She's a police inspector in the Supernatural Division of the Australian Federal Police. SUDAP, the organization is called, in the human realm. She's one of their top investigators, actually. With quite a relentless reputation."

Renna smiles just like a proud parent might.

I swallow back a derogatory retort and instead, keep my voice neutral. "She's been following up leads in relation to the abominations, and has been studying one of these medallions in their lab back in Melbourne. I thought I would take this to her, and perhaps we can pool information with the humans on this."

"Oh, no, that sounds dangerous for my children. I don't think—" Renna begins, but Rhodri cuts across her.

"I think that is an excellent idea. And I will accompany you, Tarrien."

"You, Your High...I mean, Rhodri? That will not be necessary. Indie and I can—"

"Indie and her mother can start contacting their hybrid family members, while you and I attend this... Maewen...in Melbourne." Something in the prince's voice says this is not negotiable. His next words confirm it. "So. It is decided. By royal decree, no less. We shall leave for the human realm in one hour, Tarrien. Be ready, my friend. We have work to do. People to find."

Before I can respond, his face turns murderous and he adds, "And parents to kill."

The End

I HOPE you enjoyed this second instalment in the *Blood Fae Chronicles*. Read the conclusion to this paranormal romance trilogy in *Banshee Power*, featuring Maewen and Prince Rhodri's story. Here's a sneak peek...

Maewen

I've been staring at this damn enchanted medallion for so long, my eyes are getting blurry. The vamp police sergeant, Luc Durand, handed it over after the attack in Hatton Grove, and I've been studying it in my spare moments, trying to figure out how to unlock its secrets.

Definitely infused with necromancer magic. Our calibration meter—the only one of its kind in the world designed to identify magic trace—has ascertained that much. Beyond that little snippet, the medallion has frustratingly managed to keep its own mysteries undiscovered.

The design, though, matches what we found on the bracelet of a dead necromancer last week. The guy was discovered in a back alley in the city's north, dead seemingly of a heart attack. The only reason my team was called in was because someone noticed the purple trace swirling around the bracelet. Eventually the piece of jewelry found its way here to the lab, and our trusty calibration meter ascertained it held the same trace as the medallion.

Is that how the rogue supes attacking humans are being controlled? By a necromancer "pilot"?

Yet another night is almost over, and there are still no concrete answers as to how the supernatural abominations are being controlled, nor why. Nor even *who* is behind the chaos and death.

I glance up at the clock on the lab wall and discover to my shock that it is almost midnight. Where does the time go? I need to finish up and head home, before I fall asleep right here on the floor of SUDAP's police lab in Melbourne.

The fifteen-strong members of my team already left earlier in the evening. They are generally a good bunch, accepting of having a female as their officer-in-charge. Most nights at least some of us will stay back late, depending on who caught what case, and where we're at in our various investigations, but I am invariably the last one out the door each night.

I love my job as an inspector in Australia's first national police Supernatural Division, but even I know that sometimes, I can be a little obsessive over cases that pique my interest.

I expect dedication from my team, but I don't believe in working them so hard they burn out. *No, you're leaving that fate for yourself*, my traitorous inner voice whispers.

As usual, I ignore my inner voice. She's too annoying. Though I have to admit I am far more tired than I should be, tonight. The nightmares are getting worse. I don't know how much longer I can keep taking the potion. The witch warned me there'd be consequences, but I didn't realize quite how debilitating it would be to have the little sleep I do manage to get filled constantly with dreams of death and dying.

Plus, I'm damn hungry. I don't think I've eaten since breakfast this morning. *Well*, I glance again at the clock and amend my thoughts. *Yesterday* morning.

As I put the medallion back in the reinforced glass cabinet and peel off my protective gloves and face shield, a giant yawn almost splits my face in two. Definitely time for bed.

The small lamp in my office is the only illumination left on the whole floor after I lock up the lab. I cross the hallway and head through the open-plan area where the team sits, back toward my desk. I make a mental note to ask the cleaning staff to keep the hall lights on and allow me to turn them out when I leave. No wonder my eyes are getting wonky.

I wriggle my shoulders and crick my neck, and my

stomach gives a loud rumble to remind me I need sustenance. Luckily there's a twenty-four-hour pizza place almost next door to my apartment building a few blocks from here, so I can pick up some takeout on the way home.

As I grab my bag and lean over the desk to switch off the lamp, a flash of silver light brightens the space. What the heck? I blink fast, trying to recover my vision as I scrabble for the gun on my belt. Two tall men materialize in the room.

Fae. Specifically, it is the fae warrior I met briefly several days ago—Tarrien, I believe his name was—at the cabaret club when the singer Indigo was snatched. He is accompanied by another, taller fae who I've never seen before.

My gun remains in my hand, pointing at the second man's chest before they even try to greet me. "Who the hell are you?" I demand. "And what do you want?"

"Inspector Jones, please." Tarrien shakes his head, reproach in his tone. "That's no way to greet royalty."

Royalty? The other fae inclines his head and studies me intently, as if waiting for something. Does he expect me to bow? Curtsy? Fall at his feet in supplication?

He'll be waiting a damn long time, if that's the case.

Instead I simply raise a brow, doing some waiting of my own.

To be honest, it's a bit hard to ignore how

handsome the second man is, and how much he actually does give off the air of being someone rather important. Eventually the taller fae scowls and clears his throat.

Tarrien gestures. "Inspector Maewen Jones, meet your prince. His Royal Highness, Prince Rhodri, of the Winter Court of Faerie."

My prince? I don't think so. I cock the hammer on the gun, enjoying the flicker of shock on the prince's face a little too much. *Careful, Maewen. You're over-tired. Don't play with guns. Don't tease the royal guy.*

Bet most of his subjects kow-tow to him. I can't imagine many point a gun. Especially a gun that shoots a special type of bullet comprising a mix of silver and iron.

The prince of winter would not enjoy it, should my trigger finger spasm.

Slowly I re-engage the safety and re-holster the weapon.

The wariness in both the prince's expression, and Tarrien's, reduces a notch.

"Pleasure to meet you, gents," I say. "But you haven't answered the second part of my question. What do you want? And please, make it quick. I'm hungry, and I'm tired, and I don't have an ounce of patience left in my body or my soul, tonight."

Tarrien sighs, more dramatically than I think is warranted. "What is it about Renna's children?" he murmurs.

I roll my eyes and, surprisingly, the fae prince chuckles. "He's dating your half-sister," the prince offers. "And I believe Indigo does not always do what Tarrien wants, nor expects."

The warrior shuffles his feet, obviously discomfited by the prince's explanation. A grin hovers about my lips. *Well, well. Good for you, Indigo.*

"I can also answer your query, Inspector Maewen Jones," Prince Rhodri continues.

I want to tell him it's Inspector Jones, or even just Jones, as many of the team call me. But what comes out of my mouth instead is, "Maewen. Call me Maewen, sir." *Hell.* Where did that come from?

The prince smiles—a rare one that actually reaches his eyes. Most people don't smile with their eyes. I draw in a quick breath, trying to steady myself. His effect on my senses is rather unexpected.

"Maewen," he repeats. "Such a lovely name. I insist that you call me Rhodri in return. No formality. But, you want to know why we're here. Tarrien, show her the necklace."

Tarrien pulls a plastic packet from a previously hidden inner pocket in his shirt and thrusts it in my direction. "I found this on a loup werewolf," he says. "In the Badlands, on the edge of Faerie. That's where they were holding Indie. There was a whole conclave of necromancers there. Wizards, a couple of witches, and a whole slew of rogue supes, all readying for some kind of ritual that involved draining your sister of her blood."

Slowly, I take the packet from him.

"She's fine by the way," he adds. "Thanks for asking."

I bite back a growl of annoyance. "I know, Tarrien. Indigo called me this morning and we had quite a long chat. She wants to meet soon, and I have agreed to that."

"Oh."

I manage to restrain from rolling my eyes yet again, and return to study the packet's contents. It is half-wrapped in a handkerchief, within the plastic packet, but the shape of it is obvious. "Another medallion?" I shoot him a glance, excitement punching me in the gut. Maybe this one will be easier to crack. Then a thought strikes and I frown up at him. "Did you touch it?"

"No. I used the linen handkerchief to pull it off the dead were, and then sealed it straight into the plastic. It felt...wrong, when I saw it, so I instinctively avoided touching it."

"Good." Gut instinct tells me these medallions are bad news, and I suspect things might bode badly for anyone who happens to touch one without a protective layer between. "Until we have more information about how they work, best not to touch them directly."

Prince Rhodri steps up beside me and stares down at the packet in my hand. His body imparts a pleasant warmth, creating an unexpected—and definitely unwanted—shiver down my spine.

Surreptitiously, I slide away. The prince is no fool. A wry grin is his only reaction. That man is too astute for my liking. "Thank you for bringing this to SUDAP," I say. "I'll need to lock it away with the other talismans for now, and get the team back onto it tomorrow. Hopefully we'll manage to extract some answers from them, soon enough."

"Would it help if you knew who made them?" Prince Rhodri leans against the edge of my desk, looking most un-royal-like. In his casual street clothing, he could pass for an extremely handsome human male—except for those pointed ears, and the aristocratic line of his nose, and those chiselled high cheekbones. And of course, the amazing, brilliant blue eyes that remind me of the sea on a warm summer's day... *Jesus*.

I shake my head. What the hell is wrong with me, tonight?

"It might," I say. "*Do* you know who created them?"

Tarrien clears his throat. When I transfer my attention to him, his mouth is a grim line and his eyes are flat and steely in color. "I believe it was my father."

Wait. What? "Your *father* is responsible for these medallions? But...that means..." I can't finish. The disclosure is as unexpected as it is horrifying. The trail of carnage caused by the rogue supes is a long one, over many years. I might have a deep personal dislike of the woman who birthed me, but I can't imagine what it would be like knowing your own parent is responsible for so much suffering and death.

Before I can ask *why*, Prince Rhodri speaks up, as if sensing that Tarrien isn't in the mood to admit anything else. "We think Tarrien's father created the medallions with the help of a group of necromancers. But he only did that, because he is working for my mother, formerly Queen Rhiannon of the Winter Court. She was banished from Faerie more than twenty-five years ago, but we believe she intends to try and reclaim her throne."

My mouth drops open and stays like that for a few seconds too long. Eventually, I realize I'm gaping and quickly close it. *Holy hell. We're going up against a queen of Faerie?*

To give myself time to process what Prince Rhodri has just said, I make my way around my desk and flop down into my chair, leaning back and steepling my fingers in front of my lips.

"That is a lot to take in," I manage, at last. "I assumed we maybe had a mad necromancer or two on our hands. This pushes the issue into a whole other level of concerning."

The prince nods, and leans forward over the desk, piercing me with his steady blue gaze. "We wish to join forces with you and your SUDAP team, Maewen." He smacks the top of the wooden surface with one hand. "We want to share our information, and enlist your help, so we have the best chance of locating our parents."

"And then?" I ask, meeting his gaze squarely.

His eyes light up with a fierce blue glow. "Then, Maewen," he says. "We are going to kill them."

Read more of Maewen and Rhodri's story in

Banshee Power

Blood Fae Chronicles, book 3

Then see where it all began with Aleah and Luc's story in

Banshee Cry

Blood Fae Chronicles, book 1

USA TODAY BESTSELLING AUTHOR
JEN KATEMI
BANSHEE CRY
BLOOD FAE CHRONICLES
1